WHERE THE DEAD DON'T DIE

RONALD J. MURRAY

UNCOMFORTABLY DARK HORROR

ISBN: 9798893990034

Cover Art by Don Noble of Rooster Republic

Edited and formatted by 360 Editing (a division of Uncomfortably Dark Horror).

Editor: Candace Nola

First edition 2024.

Follow UncomfortablyDark.com for the best in indie horror! Sign up for our newsletter and our Patreon!

PRAISE FOR RONALD J. MURRAY

"This raw exploration of the human psyche and relationships will bury deep beneath your skin. Murray takes readers through lyrically dark stories of labyrinths, rituals, sacrifices, and secrets. Dynamic and filled with compelling strangeness." —Sara Tantlinger, Bram Stoker Award-winning author of The Devil's Dreamland

"Where the Dead Don't Die is a disorienting fall into psychological horror that will keep you turning pages and questioning reality. This is heartbreak and anxiety trapped in beautiful prose." —Sarah Read, Bram Stoker Award-winning author of The Bone Weaver's Orchard.

DEDICATION

To Sarah, Kailo, and Caden, who keep me feeling alive.

CONTENTS

1. Jealousy   1

2. A Letter to My Future Corpse   30

3. I Have Swallowed Sin   41

4. In the Labyrinth   49

5. Cornelia   77

6. The Incident at Shore Run Road   96

7. To Taste Her Flesh   120

About Ronald J. Murray   143

Acknowledgements   144

Also By Uncomfortably Dark Horror   146

1

JEALOUSY

PART I

I DIDN'T WANT TO move until it was finished. I wasn't sure what could happen if I did. So, I just watched the water drain from the tub. I pulled my legs closer to my body and hugged them. The new inches of distance between my toes and the bathtub drain hardly served as an alleviation. This fear was new, and it was strange.

The miniature maelstrom churned above that dark mouth. I watched as it gulped with a moldy throat. A gurgle pounded against the quiet of the bathroom when the last of my water swirled away. I shuddered at the sound.

When the sizzle of soap suds that escaped the pull fell to silence, I allowed steady breathing to return to my chest. I pressed the towel against my face and exhaled deeply into the cloth. The darkness over my eyes was like a shield for a moment, but I knew I still stood in the tub. I stepped out onto the bathroom floor and shivered against the cold of the linoleum beneath the soles of my feet.

This whole room felt...*off*. Something was weird. Dreamlike. *Not real.*

I snatched the Fantasy novel I'd been trying to read in the bath from the edge of the tub, as if the drain would steal that, too—as if it wasn't just a drain and had actually stolen anything at all. What could a drain—a bathtub, a bathroom—steal? Nothing. I knew that. I ran the tips of my finger and thumb along the length of my eyebrows and then pinched the bridge of my nose.

I needed a minute to collect myself. In just a minute, this would pass, like some nightmarish *déjà vu*, and my nightly relaxation ritual wouldn't be ruined after all.

The minute passed. I allowed the subtle heat of private embarrassment to rise in my face. Afraid of the drain? I chuckled at myself. A grown adult, afraid of the bathtub. I wasn't so different from everyone else: I had a shitty job that barely paid enough to cover my outrageous portion of the rent. I had groceries to buy. I had *real life* risks and stresses that should occupy my mind, risks and stresses I was trying to escape by reading in the bath. *Afraid of the drain.* Ridiculous; *absolutely* ridiculous.

But I flashed my eyes toward the tub again. I slowly dragged my line of vision along its blue, soap scum-stained length. Long, black hairs stuck in clumps along the acrylic surface. *Not mine*, I thought, reaching to feel the orange curls of my hair. They had to have come from Reggie's head—yeah, that was Reggie's hair.

The silver faucet held my distorted reflection. I couldn't see the details of my face in it. I was a silhouette in front of the light above the bathroom mirror behind me, like a fuzzy image from a dream. I stared, and I swallowed.

Not just the drain. I blinked and barely glanced toward the bathroom door when I heard Reggie come in through the front door in the living room and toss his keys onto the end table. *Especially the drain, but the entire tub, too.* I felt the cold of the floor beneath my feet again. *The entire bathroom.*

I closed my eyes. I don't know for how long I kept them closed. I just know that I swam in the darkness behind them, in some weird bliss, knowing that I didn't have to look at my surroundings.

A fist rapidly pounded against the bathroom door. I jumped. I swung around to notice that I'd knocked my book into the bathroom sink. The leaky faucet permitted drips of water to soak into the pages along their edges before I could grab it. I winced at the sight of wet, expanding paper.

"Hey, fuckface," my roommate's deep voice boomed through the door.

"Yeah?"

"Bath time's over," he said. "It's eleven-thirty, and I gotta be up at six."

I sighed. "Alright. I'll be out as soon as I get dressed."

"Nah," he laughed. "Wrap the towel around yourself and go get dressed in your room. I need to shower."

I grunted quietly. The idea of getting my own place got sweeter and sweeter with every one of these interactions. I missed having more space than just a bedroom to define myself. I missed my house on that quiet, dead-end street. Even the dog that'd jump the neighbor's fence to harass me when I went out to work on my car had become a fond memory.

Living with Reggie wasn't like how I'd imagined it would be. He had slowly turned sour toward me. I'd begun to think of him as someone that only *used* to be a very close friend. I missed when we got along, before we lived together.

And above everything else, I missed Anastasia. I pined for her warmth next to me in our bed. Her sleeping coos, her giggles at my stupid jokes, and the scent of her tightly curled black hair haunted me. I wish I could remember why we separated; something stupid, probably. If I could find a way to convince her to take me back...

"*Riley.*" Reggie's fist pounded the door again.

"Alright, alright." I wrapped the towel around myself and turned the doorknob.

Reggie forced the door open the rest of the way and pushed past me. The pungent odor of the glistening sweat on pale skin that stretched tightly over his laborer's body maliciously swirled around my nostrils. I noticed deep red scratches slashed across his shirtless chest. His gun protruded from the waistband of his pants. He always carried that thing on him, even in his own house.

The second my foot crossed the threshold into the hallway, he slammed the door. "What the hell happened to you?" I asked.

"Fuck off."

The bathtub faucet screamed seconds later. I cringed, and I walked quickly down the hall toward my bedroom.

PART II

I sat at the edge of my chair and almost unconsciously tapped my fingertips against the surface of my desk. The taste of plastic clung to my mouth from chewing on the end of my pen. Anxiety trapped me like a prison, and this cubicle exacerbated the flames in my stomach. The fact that the internet and phone lines were down didn't help, and neither did the chatter of co-workers that banged against my ears.

I wondered if management would send us home. Maybe they liked paying their employees to sit around for hours with nothing to do but talk. Along with everything else, they seemed strange, too. Gathered behind the locked door of a conference room, they also talked for hours.

Maybe something was happening. Maybe something already *had* happened. It sure felt that way. Uneasiness clung to the air like static. I could almost taste it.

Was the haze that seemed to veil everything just a trick of my tired eyes? I blinked. The oppressive dim remained, despite the fluorescent lighting.

I shook my head and rubbed my eyes with the finger and thumb of one hand. I realized I'd been toying with the computer mouse, which awakened my temporarily useless monitors. I vibrated my lips with an exhale and reached into my pocket. The illuminated screen of my cell phone revealed no new notifications. Anastasia hadn't texted me back, and she'd returned none of the calls I'd made to her.

She wasn't a monster. I know somewhere inside her, she still cared. So why wouldn't she answer me? I just wanted to hear her voice again. I wanted to know what happened to us, and what I could do to fix it. Our separation was so sudden, and so...fuzzy in my head, distant and unrecoverable, like some memory suppressed and locked away.

Could I get her to tell me she loved me? If I could just hear it one more time, even if it did nothing but fan the fire that burned my insides, it would be worth it.

"Riley," a voice said from behind me. I heard it, but I didn't react. Something inside of me didn't let me turn around.

Please, I typed on the phone screen. *Please answer me. Please tell me what I did and why this is happening. I deserve to know.*

"Earth to Riley," the voice continued. "Wake up."

I finally turned and met the face of the girl who sat behind me. I couldn't remember her name, but I always thought she looked my sister—light brown hair that unfurled in waves and a petite, pale face that housed green eyes—so I always wanted to call her Elise. I raised my eyebrows as if to question why she'd broken my thoughts.

"Do you know what happened?" The way she asked wasn't in such a way that she was curious about anything. Her tone said that she *knew* something and was checking to see if I did, too. An ambiguous expression tugged at her facial features. I couldn't place what she was feeling. I just saw that she wasn't smiling.

"No. What?"

The girl opened her mouth to speak, but I raised my hand to stop her. My phone vibrated my palm. "I'm sorry. Give me just a second."

The name on the notification bar read *Anastasia*. She'd finally answered me.

I shot up from my chair and walked quickly toward the back hallway near the restrooms. I needed space to focus on this text message and what I would say in reply.

I tapped the screen with a shaking thumb and opened the text. My eyes traced the letters of a single word: *Jealousy.*

I drew my eyebrows inward and looked up from the screen and into the empty space around me. Jealousy? No exploration of my memories with her found any moment that either of us expressed jealousy. I never felt threatened by anyone in our circle of mutual friends or the friends she kept that I knew nothing of aside from their names and that they cared about her.

Was it someone in my life? She wouldn't kick me out if she felt as though someone *I* knew had been encroaching on our relationship. No, she'd talk to me about it, and we would have worked it out.

What do you mean? I typed in reply. *Jealousy? I don't understand.*

I stood in that hallway, outside the men's bathroom door, waiting. No reply came.

Please, I typed. I tapped send.

Another few moments. Still, nothing.

My stomach exploded, tying knots with tongues of fire. Something was wrong; terribly, terribly wrong. I needed to leave. I needed to leave *now*.

With no explanation given to my supervisors—I didn't have time to wait for them, anyway—I made my way to the stairwell through the door at the back of the hall. My feet pounded toward the bottom. They'd then pound the accelerator in my car, and I'd pray that no cops crossed my blazing path on the way to Anastasia's—*our*—house.

PART III

Reggie looked at me from across the kitchen table with furrowed brows. Two of the bulbs in the ceiling light fixture had been burnt out for some time. The dim yellow light cast shadows across his face. He looked like a nightmare, but I don't think he was angry. I think he was just concentrating on what I was stumbling to explain. He ran a hand down his face and spoke.

"No," he said, shaking his head. "I don't want anything to do with this."

"Reggie," I pleaded. "Come on, man. You've known her even longer than I have. *Somebody* needs to reach out to her, and she won't communicate with me. Something is wrong."

He folded his arms across his broad chest. "What makes you say that?" He sighed and closed his eyes for a second.

"I've been trying to get a hold of her all day. She wouldn't answer." I ran a hand through my hair and inhaled deeply. "I—I even drove to the house, and she wouldn't answer the door." I opened my eyes wider and gestured to strengthen my point. "Her car was in the driveway."

Reggie scoffed and lifted a hand from his bicep briefly. "Maybe you're coming off a little strong, Riley. There's obviously a reason she doesn't want you anymore."

I took my phone from my pocket and opened the text from earlier. "She sent me this." I slid my phone across the table.

His eyes widened and then narrowed at the screen. He lifted his head to look at me through slits.

"What the hell is she talking about? You know her and I never had any issues like that."

He forcefully slid the phone back in my direction. The corner cracked against the knuckle on my hand I'd had rested on the table. He stood from his chair.

"Can you, like, text her? Or *something*. Please." I felt pathetic begging like this, but I felt so desperate.

"I don't know, Riley. I haven't spoken to Anastasia in a month or so. You know what happened." He turned his back to me and started to walk away.

"No," I said, shaking my head. "No, I don't. I know you two had a little falling out, but I *don't* know what happened. Please, enlighten me."

He shrugged and chuckled, with his back still turned to me. "Just go get your book and take one of your fuckin' baths." He turned back around and leaned toward me, placing his balled fists against the surface of the table. "And after that, why don't you shop around for your own apartment?"

Gladly, I thought. I scowled. "You're supposed to be my friend. That's why you took me in when all this shit went south, isn't it? Why have you been acting like such an asshole towards me?"

He made a thin line with his lips and pushed himself away from the table. Without another word, he walked away. The front door slammed with his departure.

PART IV

I stood naked in the bathroom with a towel draped over my arm and a book in my hand. I took a step closer to the tub and hung the towel over the curtain rod above my head. I set my book on the edge of the tub and reached to turn the water on. The knob was ice cold. I reflexively snapped my hand away from it.

I took a step backward and turned to look at the clothes I'd folded and stacked neatly on the toilet lid. The flannel pants and oversized hoodie reminded me that I didn't have to do this. I could just put them on and go to bed.

I turned back to the tub and traced its length with my eyes. They stopped at the drain. I shook my head.

I decided I'd just read in bed, wrapped in the warmth of a comforter. Water turned cold eventually, anyway. Blankets didn't. They stayed warm and comfortable. Maybe in the morning, everything would be different.

Maybe tomorrow Anastasia would call me and tell me to come home.

PART V

"Hey. *Hey.*" The whisper broke through the veil of my sleep. "Wake up." I felt the soft sole of a cold foot touching the top of mine. It nudged me gently.

I made a noise and attempted to roll over. I wanted to sink back into the darkness that rested against my closed eyelids. A hand caught my arm and squeezed.

"Seriously," said the voice, firmer this time; louder. "Please. Wake up."

Wait. *Wait.* I knew that voice. A rush of furnace fire from the pit of my stomach found my head, and I opened my eyes to the pitch black of the bedroom. The smell was familiar, too, like a woman's hair fresh from the shower.

I extended my hand to touch the body in bed next to me. My palm found familiar curves. "Ana?"

"Riley," she said. "Riley, wake up. What is that noise?"

I concentrated, listening. A dull, rhythmic beeping played from somewhere distant in the house. The hallway, maybe? The alarm panel? Did someone open the front door? *Wait, where am I?*

"I think," the voice of Anastasia continued, "that someone is in the house. Call the police."

"What? No, no." I rubbed at my sleepy eyes that still reached for dreaming. "It's probably nothing," I said through a yawn. "That's the alert for the front door. I'll reset it from my phone. It's probably just the panel fucking up again. If someone broke in, why would they come in through the front door?"

"No, Riley. This is serious. Wake up and call nine-one-one."

I grunted and sat up and swung my legs over the edge of the bed, throwing the covers off. Using my hands to feel around in the dark, I found the light switch and flipped it. I blinked and squinted. "I'll call Guardian, then. Maybe someone can come out and replace the panel."

"Riley." Her voice was shaking, afraid.

I turned to reassure her. "I'm sure everything is—"

One ice-blue eye whirled around, looking around our bedroom with desperate fear. The other was just...not there. A thin layer of skin stretched tightly over the socket. The jet-black hair that framed her pale face dripped, soaking wet. She was naked, and the droplets of water collected along her skin glistened. The sheets beneath her were dark. Water dripped from the bed and thudded against the hardwood below.

I lurched away from the scene.

She began shaking her head. "*Call nine-one-one*," she screamed. Water poured from her mouth and nostrils. "Call nine-one-one, call nine-one-one, call nine-one-one."

I shut my eyes. With a shaken hand, I reached for the door-knob. I leaned against it to steady myself. My head whirled. It felt like the floor shifted beneath my feet. The sound of her screaming voice faded inside my head like an echo. My knees felt weak.

Everything fell quiet, save for the sound of dripping. I opened my eyes. I found myself lying in the empty bathtub. The leaky faucet permitted droplets of water to slap against the acrylic. Dark brown streaks, like dried blood, stained the blue surface of the sides and front of the tub. They trailed to the drain, where the brown built to a thicker, darker hue.

I shot upward to sit against the back of the tub. I focused on my shaken breathing, trying to calm myself. *A dream?* It felt like more: deeper, realer.

I looked at the stains in the tub, and then at my ankles. Did I thrash in my sleep and cut myself? My skin revealed no slits or gashes.

The fluorescent tube above the bathroom sink flickered dramatically to ignite a migraine pain behind my eyes. I blinked.

Something scratched from somewhere. The scraping grew loud enough to drown out the dripping. I looked around, but I knew where the sound had come from.

I leaned forward and crawled to the drain. I peered into the dark throat that swallowed comforts, that now seemingly drank blood. An eyeball rolled around, like the drain had become its socket, and it seemed to be begging to be flushed away. It looked like an iris pigmented by pale blue.

I sprang to my feet and jumped from the tub. "What the *fuck?*" I grabbed my clothes from the toilet lid and escaped the bathroom with running feet.

PART VI

Please, I typed on my cell phone screen. *Please, just tell me you're okay. I don't even care if you take me back or ever explain to me why you wanted me gone. I just need to know that you're okay.* I pressed send and leaned back in my chair. I rubbed my eyes and lifted my head to peer into the tubes of light in the ceiling.

The office was mostly empty today. Only the emergency lights illuminated the area, which accentuated the gray filter that veiled the atmosphere these days. In the mornings, before anyone from management arrived, keeping the main lights off was normal. But it was nearly noon. I checked the calendar to be sure I didn't accidentally come in on a Saturday to work with those that liked to spend their weekends getting overtime, but it was Tuesday. A holiday? No, just a regular Tuesday.

The few that occupied their cubicles kept quiet, noses buried in their work with headphones on. My assigned row only held myself and the girl that looked like Elise.

"That sounds like a hell of a nightmare," the girl that looked like Elise said from behind me. She clicked her tongue against the roof of her mouth.

"Yeah." I sighed. "Yeah, it was."

I turned my chair back around to face her, and she gave me a slight shrug. "It just sounds like," she continued, "that you're just really afraid of losing her. Your separation has really affected you."

"I don't even know why I'm opening up to you about it." I looked away for a moment, gazing down the row. "I know it'll just end up being office gossip."

"It's okay. I know what it's like to be afraid to lose someone you love." Her expression grew serious, sad. She sighed and continued. "Years ago, my brother was shot by his friend. He survived, and he's okay now. He was just comatose for a while. Shit was scary. I had nightmares about it for a long time. Still do, from time to time."

"I hope your brother isn't friends with this person anymore."

She chuckled. "Of course not. You can't really be friends with someone that shot themselves in the face after they thought they murdered you."

I realized I'd sat there wordlessly for a few moments before I replied. "Why would your brother's friend do something like that?"

She shook her head and looked away, as if thinking of something to say. "I don't know. Sometimes people that appear to be your friends really aren't. Sometimes they stab you in the back with little betrayals." She shrugged. "And sometimes they shoot you. I guess it just boils down to the fact that you have to be careful of who you allow into your life, or who you continue to allow to be a part of your life, even if they were, at one point a genuine friend."

Her words banged against the insides of my skull. I spent a long while just slouched in my chair, my fingers laced and rested on my stomach, thinking about them.

The girl that looked like Elise didn't seem to mind that I took a few minutes to process what she'd told me. She didn't turn away. She just watched the shifting expressions on my face. Then she spoke again. "So, what happened? You know, to cause a rift between you and Anastasia?"

I gave her an inquisitive look. I didn't remember telling her my wife's name. Maybe I did. Everything was swirling and confusing. A detail overlooked, I guess. "I...I honestly don't know. I've been trying to get a hold of her to find out." I swallowed hard. "Don't you think I deserve to know?"

A hint of a smile touched her lips, but it was sad. "I think you know. It's somewhere deep in there. You just have to drag it out." The smile fell away. "You have to remember, Riley."

I nodded. "I think I'm gonna head out for the day. I don't feel like I should be here." The furnace in my stomach re-ignited. My insides begged me to swing by Anastasia's again, just to check. "It's not like there's anything going on here, anyway. Barely anyone showed up."

The girl laughed. "What do you mean?"

I collided with someone when I stood from my chair. They'd been on their way down the aisle in a hurry. A stack of papers fell from their arms and scattered on the floor. "I'm so sorry," I said, bending to help them.

When I stood to hand the papers over, I looked over a brightly lit office with cubicles full of movement and work and conversations over headsets connected to office phones. Ringing and talking and the clatter of keyboards and clicking mice rattled against the walls, filling my ears.

I looked down at the girl. She sat motionless inside the sudden whirl of movement, beneath the artificial glow of rows of fluorescent tubes in the ceiling tile. Her gaze remained locked on me.

"Yeah," I said to myself beneath my breath. What in the fuck was even happening? *God, I must be cracking*, I thought. *I am definitely fucking cracking*. I then nodded to the girl and continued my goodbye. "It's definitely time for me to get out of here," I said. "Have a good day. And thanks for hearing me out and talking to me."

I walked quickly to the exit. I looked back at the scene that was invisible to my eyes just minutes ago, and then I rushed off toward the stairs.

PART VII

The front door, left unlocked, opened easily with a turn of the knob. The hinges cried to welcome me home. I didn't remember the hallway that met me on the other side, despite the years I'd lived here. I'd come home from work every day through that front door. This hallway had never been here. Long and dark, my slow and careful footsteps thudded against the hardwood as I followed its length.

The walls that closed me in, and the ceiling only inches above my head, mocked my confusion and distress with stained off-white that housed my dancing shadow. A trail of water rested between my feet, still and narrow. Curious.

"Baby?" called a distressed Anastasia. "Baby, is that you?" Her voice sounded static, as if she spoke from the other side of an old speaker.

I slowed to a stop. I stood completely still, careful not to make another sound. I listened. Would she speak again?

"Make sure you shut off that damn alarm panel."

I heard it now: that distant, rhythmic beeping. Forty-five seconds to get there and put in the code, or the police would be dispatched. I always thought the security company allowed too much time. A lot could happen in forty-five seconds.

"Riley," she called again. The static had become more prominent, further distorting her voice. "I need your help. Please. In the bathroom."

I took a slow step forward. *This isn't real.* It couldn't be. My foot crashed against the floor and the now-blaring alarm shattered the silence like glass.

Anastasia's voice played again, but backward; her words rewound like a cassette tape. Then she spoke again in a tone of anger. "It was only those couple of times!" she yelled. "I'm not—*no!*"

My pace quickened through the hallway. Shadows clung to the walls in thicker clumps as I advanced.

"What if—" She sobbed now. "*Riley!*" The scream was guttural, blood-curdling.

The silence returned while I ran. The hallway ended at a door. Cracks marred the white paint on the wood. I opened it.

On the other side, I somehow, in my own house, found myself inside the same bathroom at Reggie's place: the flickering tube above the sink, the blue tub gaping at me like a mouth that wants to swallow me, a mouth now covered almost entirely in stains of brown and clusters of black mold, and its faucet dripping and dripping and dripping. The drain groaned and scraped and scratched. The pipes shuddered beneath.

Everything seemed slow. I wanted to rub my eyes or smack myself to wake up. I was awake. Wasn't I? This was real, wasn't it? I crouched beside the tub. I touched its edge. The cold, acrylic surface against my fingertips felt real.

Real. I reached up and put my face into my palms. I squeezed my eyes shut against my fingers. I felt my hot breath bounce back against my cheeks with an exhale. *I* was real.

I saw the ghost of light in front of my eyelids flicker dramatically. A squirming, wet, slapping and sucking noise filled the quiet. My nostrils captured the copper scent of blood swirling to mingle with the pungent odor of sweat. The smell of fear and a fight.

What really *happened?*

I opened my eyes. Large, black, leech-like things filled the mouth of the tub. Wiry black hairs protruded from the large ends that I guessed were their heads. Writhing, they slipped atop one another as if in some desperate climb to escape the walls that confined them.

I wasn't afraid. I was...*numb.* Numb and cold and tired. And my eyes and head felt fuzzy.

I sat and watched their struggle. One flipped over in the mess. I swallowed and leaned closer with intrigue. A miniature human face stared back at me—Anastasia's face, a peaceful sleep fallen over it with one eye patched by a thin layer of skin.

I filled my lungs with slow and careful breath. I swallowed to drown the lump that formed in my throat and blinked away the tears that welled in my eyes.

It's somewhere deep in there. You just have to drag it out. The words echoed in my mind.

I shivered and fell to sit on the floor, wrapping my arms around my legs with my eyes still glued on the pool of creatures in front of me. Shaken breaths passed between my parted lips.

You have to remember, Riley.

Long hours passed, stretching on like blurred time that passes when you sleep through recovering from illness. I dug through my head, desperately, like one would with fingers through mud to find something precious that they'd dropped. I could produce nothing. I couldn't even remember a conversation had before leaving to live elsewhere, before leaving my wife alone. I couldn't remember anything other than that first bath to relax and read, where I'd realized my fear of the drain, the tub. When did I even start liking to take baths to relax at night, anyway? That wasn't something I'd done before going to live with Reggie.

The rattling doorknob on the white bathroom door pulled my focus away from the tub. I watched the faded and scratched brass turn, and I heard the shriek of hinges when the door finally opened.

Reggie crossed the threshold, and he looked down over me with a face full of expressionless features. He took another slow step closer to me. He loomed over me, as if to wordlessly threaten me.

My tired, bloodshot eyes met his. My gaping mouth struggled, but finally spoke. "What are you doing," I said, automatically, like I'd been spitting words into the world from the edge of a dream, "in my house, Reggie?"

He smirked and chuckled through his nostrils and took another step. He crouched to my level, and I felt his hand grip the back of my head. He squeezed a fistful of my hair in his grip.

I didn't fight it when he pushed me forward. I couldn't. It was like I'd been someone else, and I was just experiencing this assault through these eyes and this body.

The Anastasia-face leeches squirmed inches beneath my face. I wanted to gag at the smell of blood and sweat. They all turned upward and opened their mouths, begging to suck me dry. They screamed my name in a cluster of tiny, screeching wails, over and over and over.

Reggie finally submerged my head beneath the swirling, undulating mess. The leeches filled my mouth and my ears and my nostrils. I couldn't breathe. I tried to; I fought to, but the leeches just found their way deeper into my throat and my head, my lungs. I could feel them moving inside of me, *screaming* inside of me.

Everything became distant, still present in some muffled and quiet way. I stopped fighting. I just let the expanse of darkness that crept into my head wash over me. Then, nothing.

PART VIII

I'd just been lying there, looking at the ceiling, tracing the familiar cracks that split the paint near the motionless ceiling fan. My watering eyes ran tears down the sides of my head to soak the edges of my hairline. A splitting pain ran along the center of my skull. I couldn't blink it away, and sleep was a domain I'd wanted to avoid. I couldn't risk another nightmare.

Reggie hadn't been home for days. Or had it been only hours? One to be chalked up to the list of things I was no longer sure of. I could only be sure that I wasn't complaining. This time alone allowed room to rest my pounding head, to do my best to collect the scattered pieces of myself strewn across my splintering mind.

I pulled the covers closer against my skin. God, I felt like ice. I shivered.

When had I last been to work? The question pinged like an echo in the back of my head. It was for the better that I'd taken a few days off. I didn't want to ever go back. The nagging pull to go back to my house—to Anastasia's house—because I kept feeling like something horrific had happened to her had been most intense at my desk. It's not like I could get any work done, anyway. And that place was a nightmare on its own, considering my last experience there. Or was I even there? I ran my nails along the length of my face and forced an exhale between my fingers when they crossed my lips. Was I in this bed the entire time? Had everything been a dream?

I couldn't trust how real the sheets felt beneath me. I couldn't trust the cracks in the ceiling, or the bathroom, or the text on my phone that sat on the bed next to me. I couldn't trust my eyes, that told me that this was a room at Reggie's place. I couldn't trust Reggie, who drowned me in a pool of leeches with Anastasia's face in some fever-dream hallucination.

This was all a loss. I could no longer properly function. I felt like I should just kill myself. Or let Reggie kill me, if he hated me *that* much. His recent behavior sure enforced that thought.

I might as well be tied down by wires and tubes. I was done.

The front door swung open and thudded against its frame in the living room. I slowly turned my head in the direction of the sound and listened to the increasing volume of boot steps that snuck closer to me. The knob on the door to my room turned. I blinked and inhaled and accepted whatever would cross the threshold.

Reggie walked in and loomed over me. His shoulders looked broader, and his chest puffed further outward. His hands were balled into fists, and his jaw bones flared from the pressure of clenched teeth. He looked like a monster dressed in laborer's clothes.

I didn't say a word. I just looked up at him and accepted whatever was about to happen. If he killed me here and now, in this bed, I wouldn't fight it. I'd be better off dead than living a series of increasingly horrific nightmares and hallucinations, not knowing, at any moment, whether I was awake or sleeping, or just seeing things. I steadied my breathing and prepared.

He straightened and looked over me with narrowed eyes. "Why did you go there?" He spoke with a firm tone. "You know you shouldn't have."

I looked up at him with half-closed eyes. I spoke with a voice that was half-there, slow, slurred, and sleepy. "Go where? What do you mean?"

He scoffed. "You fucking know what I mean. You went to Anastasia's."

"No, I didn't. That was a dream."

He leaned over me, placing his fists next to me on the mattress. "I fucking saw you there. I was there. Wake up, Riley. She doesn't want you anymore. Leave her alone." He stood again and laughed, looking somewhere past me. He looked at the wall, maybe. Or maybe he looked out the window next to my bed.

"And now they know. Because you went there, and now you know. They know now."

I rolled to my side and sat up half-way, putting my weight on one elbow. I furrowed my brows and dug into Reggie with my eyes. "Who knows what? What are you talking about? I don't understand."

He sighed through his nostrils. "They know." He paused. "And you know. You know that she's mine now." He looked down at me again. "She's mine now. Forever and always, just as I always wanted it to be." His eyes had become glazed over. The caricature of a peaceful smile tugged at the corners of his mouth.

"I guess that makes you mine now, too. In a way." He shrugged. "It's why you're here, after all."

"She's yours now?" My head whirled. I pinched the bridge of my nose. "Who knows? What?"

"*They* know. And it's because you saw it." The pitch of his voice became higher. He spoke faster. "You saw her becoming mine. And you told them."

I heard the front door burst open like an explosion. A cluster of boots slammed against the floor and moved throughout the house in a swift mess of thuds. Calm but hasty shouts shot through the air like bullets. "In the bathroom, in the bathroom," a deep voice yelled urgently to the others.

Three gun-wielding, armor-clad police officers burst through my bedroom door. One kept their gun fixed on Reggie while the others tackled him to the floor. I blinked, and he was on his stomach, hands cuffed behind his back.

They didn't notice me.

As they dragged Reggie away through the door, I swung my legs over the edge of the bed. I stood and crossed the floor.

In the bathroom. In the bathroom, echoed in my head.

I pushed the bathroom door open. Blood streaked from the side of the tub to pool onto the tile floor. The floor of the tub itself had seemingly fallen in on itself, leaving a gaping hole— a mouth to breathe hot air at me. The faint sound of thudding feet and grunting and splashing and crying poured from the throat.

I stood over the opening. My gaze could not tear through the thick, material black of the abyss beneath me. With one leg, I tested its depth. My foot touched no surface as I straddled the edge.

I swung my other leg over and sat on the edge. I looked at my feet, dangled over the blackness. I hesitated and inhaled deeply. A few inches forward, and I descended with a quick fall.

PART IX

I'd found a narrow hallway with some impossibly high, unseen ceiling hidden by shadows waiting for me at the bottom. My body slapped against a wet floor, sending droplets of water shooting upward at my face. A deep echo bounced the sound back toward me. My eyes hurt when I tried to peer through the black that enveloped me.

I took my phone from the pocket of my slacks—a piece of the business casual work clothes I knew I hadn't been wearing in bed moments ago—and found the flashlight app in the drop-down menu. I began traversing the length of the hall by the light with slow and uncertain steps.

On either side of me, a sculpted image of my own face patterned the walls like a sick collage. A neutral expression painted stone-white features, and the eyelids were closed as if in peaceful sleep. I tried not to look at them after my first examination, deciding it would be best to just keep my head forward and press on.

The shallow stream of water that covered the width of the floor began rushing toward me in intermittent spurts. I imagined a coughing mouth expelling water from lungs.

I heard the distant, muffled sound of squealing hinges. A gasp vocalized. Then, a splash. Everything sounded as though it played from a tape reel, all around me; echoey, staticky and above me, behind me, beside me. But only darkness and walls patterned by my sleeping face and the water on the floor accompanied me. I slowed my pace and focused on listening.

My ears perked. I nearly stopped in my tracks. "What the hell?" said Anastasia's terrified voice. "What are you doing here?" Sloshing accompanied her words, as if she quickly moved in a small pool of water.

"Sorry to interrupt your reading," Reggie's chuckle echoed. "I'm here to see you, babe. Why else would I be here?"

"While I'm bathing? You just came into my house, unannounced, without knocking?"

"Come on." Reggie laughed. "It's not like I haven't seen you naked before. And of course. I thought we were close enough that I could just come in. What's the problem?"

"Just..." She sighed. "Just get out."

"No, come on. Let me in there with you." I heard the clang of a belt buckle come loose.

"Reggie. Get out of my bathroom. Get out of my house!"

"Oh, Ana. Calm down. It's not like we haven't done this before."

More sloshing echoed. "That was only those couple of times, and they were a mistake. And we can't do it again. It's wrong, Reggie. It's wrong. It's not fair to Riley. What if—"

He laughed loudly. "If you really loved Riley, you wouldn't have fucked me those times. So, does it even really matter?"

"Yes," she replied firmly. "It does matter. It really does."

I stopped walking. My stomach twisted. I wanted to throw up. I couldn't believe what I was hearing.

"Are you gonna tell Riley about us, then?"

"There is no *us*. There were a couple of drunken nights that ended in mistakes when Riley wasn't around, and they were wrong. Now, *please*. Leave. Leave before I call the police."

"But I—I love you, Anastasia. I can give you so much better."

"No, Reggie. Listen to me. I love Riley. There is nothing here, nothing between us. Now, get out. *Get. Out.*"

Reggie made a noise that sounded like a trembling exhalation through his nostrils. "No. No, I won't. You're fucking mine, and you need to realize that."

"I'm calling the police."

"Put your fucking phone down."

My phone vibrated my palm. The back light ignited the screen. A push notification appeared: a text from Anastasia. It read, *Riley, I need you home now. Hurry! Help.*

I ran. The narrow darkness stretched into material shadow ahead. I had no idea where this hall ended. My legs couldn't carry me along its length quickly enough.

I heard flesh smack against flesh. The sound of a fist connecting with skin. Anastasia sobbed. Knuckles slammed flesh again. And again. Water splashed.

"Please, Reggie," she cried.

His only reply, from what I could hear, came as a sharp inhalation through clenched teeth. Then he grunted.

"*No—*" Her shout had been abruptly cut off. Another splash. Sloshing. The sounds of a struggle.

I ran harder. My lungs burned. The light of my flashlight strobed with my bouncing and swinging arms. I prayed I would get to the end of this hall soon. If this hall ended at all, of course.

It did. I nearly tripped and fell forward when I skidded to a stop. I nearly turned and ran the other direction when my head processed what I was looking at.

The hallway didn't end with a door or a wall. I stopped at a towering version of Anastasia's face. I had to run my flashlight upward to see her expressionless entirety. One eye remained closed, while the other had been sealed by that thin layer of skin.

Massive, chapped lips trembled, then moved to form words. "Riley." The wind of her whisper felt hot against my body. Her breath smelled like rot and mildew.

"It's time to wake up now."

One eye opened to look down at me with an icy blue gaze. Her mouth opened wide to spill water toward me. I was met with a dark tunnel where her throat should have been. I hesitated. I didn't want to step further.

But I knew I had to. So, I did.

Everything felt like a memory, or a dream, when I reached the end of the darkness and opened a white door. I found myself in the bathroom in my home when I closed the door behind me. It was identical to the bathroom at Reggie's. Or the bathroom I *thought* was at Reggie's.

The alarm system blared, but it sounded distant and muffled. Everything moved quickly, blurry. But it all felt slow, and I felt panicked and helpless and sick and like my insides were on fire—*really* on fire with the white-hot flames of terror and anger.

"*What the fuck are you doing?*" I screamed.

Reggie crouched over the bathtub. The muscles in his shirtless back flexed as he applied downward pressure to a flailing Anastasia.

I dropped the cell phone, which already had an open line with nine-one-one, on the floor. I rushed at him. My balled fists had no effect on him as they collided with his back and the back of his head.

Anastasia's naked body fell still and pale and dead. Her limbs floated to the surface of the water. The book she'd been reading floated in the tub beside her. Blood trailed to the tile floor from the edge of the blue acrylic tub. The blood had obviously come from her eye, which had since swollen completely closed.

Reggie turned toward me. He reached for the gun that he always kept in the waistband of his pants. He pulled it and pointed it at me. His face contorted. His skin was almost tinged purple, and veins pulsed in his forehead. Tears poured from his eyes. "She was supposed to be mine," he said. He pulled the trigger.

I fell to the floor. I clutched my stomach. My skin became quickly coated in my blood. I writhed and screamed in searing pain until weakness and stillness took me.

Reggie appeared to stand over me. His silhouette blurred and came into focus. He pointed the gun at me again. This time, he took aim at my face.

I heard the front door burst open. A cluster of feet pounded on the hardwood floor in the living room.

Reggie turned the gun upward and placed the barrel beneath his chin. I watched him pull the trigger. I saw his blood and brain matter paint the white of my bathroom ceiling.

The white of the flickering fluorescent tube above the sink got brighter and brighter and brighter. My vision became filled with burning white light.

PART X

I don't remember closing my eyes, but I must have, because I opened them. When I did, my vision was assaulted with more bright white. I found myself staring at a light fixture in a white-tiled ceiling.

Pain tore through my body. My skin felt irritated, and the coarse white fabric beneath me and covering me didn't help. Rhythmic beeping played from somewhere beside me, and I realized it was the sound of a machine that monitored my heartbeat.

I was lying in a hospital bed.

"Please stay awake this time, Riley," said a familiar female voice from beside me. "Please, please, please."

I couldn't turn my head, but I moved my eyes and strained to look. Elise sat in a chair next to my bed. Her face lit up, a smile pushing her cheeks into puffs, when she saw that I looked at her.

I couldn't speak. I tried. My lips barely moved, and I made some strange, throaty sound when I tried to vocalize my thoughts. I wanted to tell her I remembered—that I knew what happened. I wanted to tell her I got a text from Anastasia, telling me to come home. I wanted her to know I remembered rushing home from work and finding out that the man who was supposed to be my best friend murdered my wife because he was jealous and crazy. I wanted to cry to her that I wish I'd known so I could have prevented this tragedy. I wanted her to tell me that, even though I couldn't turn back time and change the past, everything would be okay one day.

Elise stood up. She gently placed her hand on my arm. "I'll go get the nurse! Or—or the doctor! Hang on!"

I watched her run from the room and into the hallway outside the door, shouting excitedly for a nurse.

I took a breath, and I felt how real the air was that filled my lungs. I felt how real the raging fire in the pit of my stomach was. I wanted to ball my fists and spit flames and smoke with a grinding, angry scream.

2

A Letter to My Future Corpse

PAINTINGS HAVE THEIR STORIES to tell. The scattered, marked canvasses around this room told the spiderweb of mine. They helped me remember the things I have seen in the dark, and they asked those solemn shadows to reveal their own secrets. Every finished piece held the resounding footsteps toward the elusive answer to the question of who I am.

The scratch of dry brushstrokes itched the surrounding silence. The chemical scent of acrylic paint opened the door to a short serotonin burst. Shadow blended into the icy depiction of dead flesh, an almost marbled mixture of pale blues and white that spoke of the early stages of decomposition. Stringy gray hairs remained intact, connected to a flaking scalp, slack jaw and chin, and to cheeks that rose toward sunken eye sockets, collapsed in on themselves with the weight of reality. And I realized the fear of dying before the old and crooked fingers of my future corpse could grasp the answers I sought.

I sighed and leaned back on my stool to study my painting from a slight distance.

The corpse, seated upright in a chair, cradled a bundle of blankets. The shape of small arms and legs formed against the fabric that obscured a baby's face. I smiled softly at this representation of infantile existence: formless other than new human, ready to be molded.

I stood and walked to the kitchenette to wash my brushes. Along the way, I scanned the canvasses leaned against the wall, and I wasn't sure if my gaze held admiration for my previous work or inquisition of what they meant to me as I created them. A mouthless mannequin looked back at me with eyelids sealed by eternal sleep. A spider hung in its web, circular patterns painted onto the upper side of its abdomen.

When I passed the end table next to the futon, the digital face of the alarm clock, placed next to a photo frame I'd long torn a memory from, glowed red with 2:57 AM. I knew I had to hurry. The night wouldn't wait for me.

I stroked and separated bristles beneath the warm flow of water. Hues of black and blue and red and brown bled into the drain, swirling with a final goodbye. I set my brushes on the stainless-steel surface and sighed as the three o'clock alarm buzzed.

I turned the knobs on the faucet. The water stopped. And I returned to my living room where I killed the lights and placed the clock facedown. I sat on my futon.

I waited, peering into the pitch black in front of me. Long moments passed like ghosts. I filled the silence with rumination.

Important things were often lost because we've lost ourselves in them. But that makes the most important loss the one of ourselves. Which made me question if I had ever really found myself in the first place? The thought weighed more heavily on me tonight.

What makes, I thought, *a person whole?*

I remembered good times. Good times with *her*. The memories came automatically, and they fought harder to stay if I pushed against them. Her laughter, fresh as ever, played like a swarm of locusts. The white of her smile beamed like fangs licked clean to chew my heart.

Not that. I knew that, in a way. Did I really have a full understanding? Companionship doesn't make a person whole. But the fact that I obsessed over the loss told me that I didn't really get it.

She lightly beat her palms against my chest in my memory. Her enthusiastic voice echoed. The sound pierced my stomach and twisted.

I allowed tears to roll down my cheeks. Quiet sobbing knew no stifling gate with me. The fear of bottling my emotions, like I have so many times, kept me from really stopping them.

Her face twisted. She closed a fist. She wound up. She swung. As her knuckles made their impact in my mind, I felt real, hot breath graze the back of my neck. The floor creaked behind me. I tried not to jump—I really did. But I couldn't help it. I did.

The night had begun.

The dark had never given me light until this night. A sliver of yellow glow appeared beneath the door across the room. It stretched a distance along the hardwood before shadow found victory against it.

I squinted until I saw the knob. But I stayed reluctant to get up and open the door. Not yet.

Another hot exhale danced through the little hairs on the back of my neck. I clenched the cushions beneath me and felt my face twist, my stomach turn.

I opened my mouth. "Show me," I whispered. "I'm ready."

The memory persisted. She bared her teeth. She grabbed the floor lamp that stood in the corner near our front door by the stem. She shook it. She slammed it against the wall. Glass shattered and scattered like shrapnel.

I squeezed my eyes shut. I sucked air through my teeth and forced spit between them with a sobbing exhale. "Get out of my head," I grated. I clenched my jaw harder. My scalp shrieked as I pulled a fistful of hair.

She blocked the doorway. She pushed me into a room. "This isn't over," she growled. An open palm slammed against my cheek.

I thought of my mom. My brother. My sisters. A text would bring them to me. To get me. To save me. Even if my car keys stayed in her possession. There would be salvation. But my phone was watched. She would know.

"I want to know *me*," I cried into the darkness. "Not remember what happened." Fear clung to the back of my mind with unrelenting claws and swelled. I wondered if I'd ever be able to separate my identity from those years of hell that slept inside me.

Slow, grated breathing whispered into my ear. I felt phantom fingers glide along my shoulders. A ghostly hand tingled my forehead with its touch.

Where I knew floor stretched beneath my feet felt as though it'd fallen away into bottomless nothing. I leaned forward and fell into the dizziness that swirled inside my skull.

I groaned and closed my eyes.

I heard a voice whisper, but I couldn't understand the words.

When I opened my eyes, I was sprawled on the floor in front of the futon. The afternoon light filtered in through the blinds.

Therapy came and went as those sessions usually did. Three appointments per week tended to blend together. I'd been trying to apply the tactics my therapist suggested to me, but they were difficult to remember. I kept meaning to bring a notebook and write them down, but my head seemed too jumbled to keep any simple task straight.

I finally told my therapist about these late-night experiences, and she thanked me for my honesty. After satisfying her that I'd been taking my daily cocktail of medications as directed, she chalked them up to nightmares congruent with my diagnosis: complex PTSD.

"They're too vivid," she'd said, "for them to be manifestations in the way you're describing them. They don't work that way. You'd only see shapes by just looking into the dark. You wouldn't be feeling anything physical from that. They're just very vivid dreams that seem real." She tapped her pen against her lips like she always did to signify she wasn't done talking. "At worst, you're experiencing some hallucinations, but I doubt it. Regardless, we won't rule it out."

Everything she said made sense from a scientific standpoint, but she didn't understand how real these experiences had been. I decided that I wouldn't be bringing them up to her again. When she would undoubtedly ask, I'd just lie.

The decision was made that I'd be more closely monitored. If things got too bad, I'd be hospitalized again, and the events in my life might culminate in more diagnoses. I needed to be careful.

The sun began to fall asleep somewhere behind nearby buildings that cast their long shadows over my home. By the time I'd set up my easel, my eyes burned from the distraction of another all-day low-budget horror movie marathon and an interesting YouTube video about the psychology of spiders. What stuck out to me most in the latter was that a direct expression of their consciousness could be found in their webs.

The cracked door I imagined came to life on the canvas in painted areas of black and brown. A right angle of soft yellow created light to pour into the shadowy room. I wondered what the other side of the threshold held for me. If I were brave enough, I would find out.

A flash of my eyes to the clock reminded me that I needed to finish up. I washed my brushes and turned off the lights before I sat on my futon again to wait.

The night arrived with a floorboard creak and the breath on my neck. I shivered it away and shut my eyes.

Rumination emerged again. A pattern I had little control over. The chain that connected who I was to a person from my recent past, and the things that happened there, snapped tight. And if I fought against my shackles, the bond seemed that much more unbreakable.

A fire re-ignited in my stomach to stoke the memories.

She sang *Brown-Eyed Girl* in the passenger seat while I drove her SUV. I reached over and gently placed my hand on her thigh. She pushed my touch away.

I analyzed the memory as if I could change it. I asked myself whether I had done things differently if things would have turned out the same. I knew I wasn't perfect. I knew there were times I'd used words like a knife—in psychological self-defense; I am told by my therapist—and the result was always more complex abuse.

She grabbed my hand and gently caressed my forefinger with her thumb. "I'm sorry," she said. Her soft tone bathed me in the comfort of knowing that the moment had passed and the thought that maybe things would be different now.

The image shifted. I watched myself sitting on the end of the living room couch near the doorway that led to a hall. I bent forward to place my forehead into my palm. An argument had ended minutes ago, and I'd only wanted to take time to let the anger simmer and eventually extinguish.

She sneaked quietly behind me from the doorway. Her face contorted with rage. She closed her fist and swung. Her knuckles slammed against the back of my head. Light filled my vision for a split second and then dissipated.

She ran through the front door to return a minute later with open arms. She wrapped me in her embrace and tangled her fingers in my hair to massage the pain away.

I deserved it.

The thought must have triggered the things in the room with me. The breathing at my neck slowed and stopped. I felt fingers rest on my closed eyelids.

Are you sure about that? The whisper traveled between my ears. A voice layered with different tones: a child, a man, my mother, something that was none of those.

Then I felt like something more than sleep grabbed me, as if it were going to suck me through the futon, through the floor, and into some void.

I awoke on the floor like I usually did after those nights, and I went through the motions of my eventless day until it was time for another therapy session.

Only the little lamp on her desk illuminated her office, the overhead florescent tubes sleeping. I enjoyed the dim atmosphere and asked her if we could keep this comfortable lighting for my sessions from now on. She agreed and dug into our work.

"You know," she replied to something that I said. "Identities are a complex thing. It's hard to keep pinned down exactly who we are, because we're ever shifting. It's what makes us human."

"That doesn't explain why my mind is so fixated on my recent break-up, though." I sighed and looked down. "It's honestly just getting in the way."

"But it *does* explain why you're so fixated on that." She gently chuckled. "That was a major thing that happened in your life. She made big mistakes that greatly impacted you, and you likely did the same to her. It wasn't *right* that it happened, but it happened." She pointed at me with the tip of her pen. "And you're trying to work what happened into your identity."

What she said hit me like a knife. "But it was just a relationship." And I know I also fucked up. But she was right: it wasn't right, but it did happen.

"It was. For years. And relationships with other people are probably the most important part of our lives. They continually shape us. Don't write it off as invalid."

I didn't reply. I wanted to allow myself the time to let her words swim in my head, and she permitted me my moment.

"Life is a series of small deaths." She continued. "And rebirths from them. Think of it this way: you're still that blank mannequin from your painting you showed me, ready to be dressed in the new clothes of a new day. And you're still that spider, sitting in the center of its web. You just haven't figured out how to work this newly born part of you, which is coming into the world kicking and screaming, into the complexity of your web yet."

I allowed my gaze to trail away from hers. Images shifted in and out of my head. I wondered what was in store for me tonight. And if I could keep her words close.

She broke my thoughts. "Are you still having those dreams?"

———◆○◆———

THE ALARM BUZZED MINUTES ago. Brushes had been washed. The clock face had been pressed against the wood of the end table. And the lights had been killed.

I sat on my futon, waiting. Blinking until my eyes could adjust to the dark again.

The floor creaked behind me. Something dragged along the carpet.

I dug my fingernails into the fabric of the futon. The muscles in my back tensed, and I felt an uncomfortable shift in the skin of my shoulders.

The light under the door came.

The scraping stopped somewhere nearby.

Heat and chill rose in me at once. My skin felt like it wanted to rise from my bones.

A click sounded from the door, and it popped open a crack. Light spilled into the room to reach toward me. A scent that reminded me of roadkill, but much heavier and stronger, accompanied the light with its own creep.

I blinked my widened eyes when I noticed the porcelain white shape in my peripheral vision. I turned my head. The mannequin stood deathly still beside me.

Oh, fuck. My shaken breathing broke the quiet. I tried to steady myself with deep inhales and long exhales. In through my nose, out through my mouth. But the tremor in my body persisted.

Dry plastic squealed against itself as the mannequin bent at the waist. Its mouthless face stopped inches from my own. I glanced sideways to look at its closed eyelids.

I slowly curled my fingers against my legs. I dug my thumb against my flesh in an effort to soothe myself. These visions had never been so vivid. The fear that churned in my stomach and crawled throughout my body could have been tangible. My ears filled with the sound of my heartbeat.

Another squeal. A plastic palm rested above my lap.

I looked down.

Soft, white, silky strands stretched between motionless plastic fingers. A small spider fervently weaved a web. Its black, spiny legs moved to connect the mess of its creation. The creature would soon rest in the center of its web, its home.

My concentration on the arachnid's artwork brought me a sense of calm. I noticed my breathing had become regulated again.

"I am built of the webs I weave," I whispered. What I take from my past relationships, and what I learn from new ones; what I do and where it leads me, and what I decide to do with new skills and connections; all these things create me, and I could create myself through conscious decision.

The mannequin's eyes snapped open. Plastic eyeballs fell from its sockets into my lap.

The door opened wider. Light bathed my face.

I slid my lap from beneath the mannequin's hand and stood from the futon. I rolled the eyeballs in my hand and walked toward the light of the doorway to cross the threshold.

A hallway stretched in front of me. Yellow light from a bulb in the cornered ceiling bathed the aged paper on angled walls and the stained hardwood of the floor. The stench of rot swam through the atmosphere of the enclosed space.

A bloated corpse sat against the triangular wall at the dead end of the hallway, cradling an infant concealed by blankets. An exact image from my painting.

I covered my mouth and nose and stepped forward lightly.

Two flies emerged from inside the corpse's head, flying away from each hollowed eye socket.

I held my breath and leaned forward. I rolled the eyeballs in my palm again. Then I cautiously, hesitantly, *nervously* placed them into the corpse's eye sockets.

The blanket moved. My breath hitched. I lurched away.

The newborn wailed with a fresh cry.

I stared for what felt like forever. Tears welled in my eyes. I sighed and let them fall freely down my face to pool along my fingers.

I am made of the webs I weave.

My soft crying broke into sobbing.

I curled up on the floor by the corpse's feet. I listened to the baby's cry until exhaustion took me, sweeping me away into the void of sleep so I could meet the new morning reborn.

3

I HAVE SWALLOWED SIN

I TOOK MY MEDICINE today; it'll make me lovable. I just have to remember to take it every day. That's the part I have trouble with. And I took a deep breath because breathing keeps me calm. In through my nose and out through my mouth, like the therapists told me to do.

I paced the perimeter of the room, flashing my eyes to the crawlspace door each time I passed it. The corner of my composition notebook journal peeked at me from under the door. I kept my journal in there because I didn't want anyone to read it. I got frustrated every time I saw that speckled black and white piece of the cover. I tried to remember to kick it all the way under, but each time I found myself in the other corner of the room, I realized I'd forgotten. After grating a little grunt, I'd breathe deep and try to remember for next time.

I gently ran my fingers along the length of the green wall of the empty room, listening to the echo of my footsteps against the hardwood. Uncle Geoff said we could begin furnishing the space when he got home. He said he'd get a futon, an entertainment stand, and a television. We'd stuff it all in here, and, since I really took a shine to this room ever since we first got here, it could be my very own room. I could finally stop sleeping on the couch downstairs, and I was excited.

I looked out the one window in here and down to the main road that split Monongahela, Pennsylvania in half. And I wondered when he'd be home. I wondered what had kept him so long.

Maybe he'd decided to just leave me here, fed up with all my "stuff," as he'd called it. "I can't deal with you when you're doing all this *stuff*," he'd said when he was fed up with me before he left today.

It's not that I'm *crazy*. Even Uncle Geoff never told me that I was crazy, even if it felt like he *wanted* to say that a lot of the time. I just had a lot of feelings bottled up inside me. They made me kick and scream when they bubble up and decide they were coming out. Sometimes I'd scratch at my own arms. I had little scars here and there from when the feelings got *real* bad. That's when Uncle Geoff took me to see the doctors so they could give me medicine.

Genevieve didn't like that I took the medicine. She made that very clear when I told her the last time she visited. "You have swallowed sin," she'd said when I told her I had to take it. I remember I wrote that down in my journal: *I have swallowed sin.* I thought it sounded interesting.

"If you want the bad feelings to go away," she continued. "You have to pray to God to take them away." If I'd be a good kid, God would answer my prayers.

I guess all the churches in this town made her really believe in God. I didn't get it; things were so much different in Chicago. But it wasn't my place to tell anyone what to believe. I'd just humor her when she'd say things like that.

I tried to explain to her that I wasn't a kid. I am sixteen. That meant I was almost an adult. But she didn't believe me. I didn't know how old she was, but she had a small voice, and she must have thought everyone was a kid if she said I was a kid. (I mean, I have to *shave* now. Come on!) So, she must have been a kid herself.

She would probably be visiting again soon. That made me nervous.

I hugged myself and walked a little faster. I realized I'd dug my fingernails into my arms.

Breathe. Breathe. Slowly.

I inhaled through my nostrils for five seconds. I exhaled through my mouth for seven.

I concentrated on the feeling of my feet against the floor as I walked.

Heel. Toe. Heel. Toe.

I liked Genevieve, but I didn't like the other things she'd said to me when she found out about the medicine. I couldn't tell Uncle Geoff what she'd said, or else he'd tell me she wasn't allowed to visit anymore or something. He already didn't like her and often told me just to ignore her when she talked to me.

He told me she wasn't real. But I knew she was real. Even other people knew her. She was kind of famous. They talked about her on that cool little candlelight tour we went on in October. So, I don't understand how he could tell me that she wasn't real.

"Bad feelings are a like a virus," she said. "And daddy told me that medicine can't take away a virus. Only God can, if he decides to."

"But Uncle Geoff says this will work like an antibiotic. I just have to take my prescription and it'll make me feel better after a little bit of time."

She made a growly noise with her throat. "Your uncle tells you mean things, too."

"He doesn't mean those things that he says. He just gets frustrated."

"My daddy said he didn't mean the things he said either." She made a *humph* noise, and I imagined her shrugging. "But I hurt him, and now he's not allowed to leave the chair downstairs by the window."

They talked about the man in the window on the tour, too. I didn't know that was Genevieve's dad until she told me.

"I don't like the things Uncle Geoff tells me sometimes," I said. "But that doesn't mean he needs to be hurt."

"If he keeps being mean to you, I'll hurt him. I'll tell him he's not allowed to leave wherever I decide to put him."

The threat made me worried and sad. I remember sitting on the floor by the crawlspace door and crying after she left that day. I tried not to think about it, but I replayed the time she said that again and again in my head.

Heel. Toe. Heel. Toe.

Breathe.

Loosen your fingers, I thought. *You're digging into your arms again*. I could still feel a small burning on my skin from earlier today.

The sun began to set. I could tell because the shadows in the room started to blend in with the growing dark. I wondered how much longer Uncle Geoff would be gone. He didn't say when he'd be back, so I didn't know when to expect him. I started to get more nervous as time went by.

I reminded myself to loosen my grip on my arms again with a look at my fingers and a little nod. My slow exhale shook.

I looked out the window, but I couldn't see his truck. So, I continued my walk around the edges of the room, and I continued waiting.

The door thudded downstairs.

A knot of excitement tied itself together in my belly. I guess Uncle Geoff had finally come back.

Footsteps thudded up the stairs outside my room.

I wanted to rush to open the door, but I didn't want to scare Uncle Geoff. So, I waited for him to come to me.

I couldn't wait to see what this room looked like with all those things. I'd given a lot of thought to what I'd watch first on my new television. Too many movie titles whirled in my head, so I couldn't decide which. Maybe I'll just pick one of my favorites at random.

I inched closer to the door, waiting for it to open.

Something scratched against the ceiling, and I knew then that Uncle Geoff had not yet come home.

Genevieve had come to visit me. I knew that her favorite way to go around this room was by walking on her hands on the ceiling. She liked the noise her fingernails made when she dug them into the paint.

"Boo!" She said, her mouth inches from my ear. I imagined her neck stretching out long and thin until her head met mine. She skittered around with scratches.

"You didn't scare me!" I exclaimed.

She giggled.

"I heard you come in."

"Did you take your medicine today?"

"I have to, Genevieve. Uncle told me they'd make me feel better."

She made a grinding, throaty sound. "I told you not to."

"I know you did, but I have to. I have to listen to him, and I have to listen to my doctors."

"Sinner." The word hissed from her mouth like a scratchy whisper. "I told you what to do."

"I know," I said, my tone of voice a little sheepish. "I don't know if I want to do that."

"Why not?"

"I don't know if I want to believe in God or pray to him. And I asked Uncle Geoff about it. He said I don't have to if I don't want to."

The scratching noises slowed. I could almost feel her piercing gaze on the back of my head.

"He said it would be better if I just stick to the science and listen to the doctors, anyway."

A long scratch crossed the ceiling. A loud thud banged against the wall on the opposite side of the room. I knew she kicked the wall. She did that sometimes when she was mad.

"I—I'm sorry, Genevieve."

"Only God can remove your sickness. The virus will spread if you keep swallowing sin."

"But—"

"I know he said mean things to you today."

"How? You weren't here."

"Yes, I was. I watched through the window."

I looked over at the window. She must have climbed the outside of the house to look in here.

"You were kicking and screaming and scratching yourself."

I swallowed. I didn't want to hear about the things I do when I'm upset. I get sad to know that I have such bad feelings.

"You hit him when he tried to hug you, and he swore at you." Her voice came from beside my ear again. I felt the chill of her cold breath on my neck. "He told you he couldn't take it when you were like this. He told you to take your medicine. You wouldn't be lovable if you didn't take your medicine, he said. I heard him."

"Stop it, Genevieve." I covered my ears and closed my eyes and took a deep breath. I crouched and then sat. I focused on the feeling of my butt against the floor. I tried as hard as I could to taste the air that I sucked into my nostrils.

"Where is your uncle now?"

"He's out. He's getting furniture and a television for me." I paused. I blinked. I looked at the corner of my journal poking out from the crawlspace. "Why? Are you going to hurt him?"

She giggled. "He said mean things to you."

"He doesn't mean them."

"Plus, he reads your journal."

"No, he doesn't." I scowled at the corner I'd last heard her voice come from. "He wouldn't do that to me."

"Yes, he does. I've seen him reading it." She sighed. "You better find a better hiding place."

I looked again at the journal.

"Hurry. Before he comes home."

Quickly, I crawled over to the crawlspace door. I went so fast that I kept banging my knees off the hardwood. They hurt, and I worried that I might have bruises on them soon.

I gripped the little knob on the door and stopped before I turned it. "Are you lying to me, Genevieve?"

"He reads it. I'm telling you."

I swung the crawlspace door open. I looked inside as I almost dove to grab my journal. I stopped.

I peered into the little room, and what looked like a heap of clothing met my gaze. A flannel shirt, checkered with blue and yellow, and a pair of denim jeans curled on the floor. The soles of a pair of shoes faced me. "Uncle Geoff?" I said quietly. I looked harder and saw a face wrapped in shadows. Half-closed eyes and empty eyes peered at me from the dark.

"Genevieve!" I screamed. "Did you hurt him? He's not moving!"

She giggled again. "He's not allowed to leave the crawlspace now."

She scratched across the ceiling.

"Why would you do this?" I breathed through my teeth, fighting tears that won. "I asked you not to hurt him."

She didn't answer.

I sat against the wall until the sun became the moon. I slid the pen from the cover of my journal and removed the cap, and I crawled to where the moonlight put a window-shaped light on the floor.

I looked again into the crawlspace. It was too dark to see if Uncle Geoff was still in there.

I opened my journal, but I couldn't write. Words didn't matter anymore. It was only me and Genevieve now.

4

IN THE LABYRINTH

A MAZE OF PLEASURE. That's what the club looked like to Mitchell. He just had to navigate his way to a night of fun beyond these walls.

He forced his way through the crowd with an assertive politeness to lean his elbows against the bar. He allowed the bartender to notice his eyes that scanned the curves of her waist. They traced back upward to where her petite breasts strained the slit of the tight fabric between them, and finally they met the sharp-featured face that was framed by straight brown hair. She produced a robotic customer service smile.

"Not a chance, Mitch." Her tone rang firm. "I know your situation, whether you left your ring at home or not."

Mitchell cracked a smile at the girl. "Actually, it's in the car," he said, laughing a bit. "Can't have her *knowing* that I went to the bar without it. But you know, Marissa, what she don't know, don't hurt her." He smirked and shrugged.

Marissa's expression had quickly twisted from amused to dour. "I said no."

"Alright, alright." He showed his surrendering palms.

"What are you getting?"

His eyes flashed to the blackboard above the bar where black-light reactive chalk listed common drinks and foods. He squinted for a moment before making his decision. "Uh," he mouthed, drawing out the sound. "Give me The Kraken."

"The Kraken?" Marissa raised her perfectly plucked eyebrows, her large green eyes widening. "Powerful stuff. Enough of those, and you won't be able to perform. I mean," she laughed. "If you can get anybody to leave with you tonight."

He gave her a smug look. "Or it'll boost my already ever-present confidence."

She rolled her eyes. "You mean *arrogance*." She grabbed a few bottles from the shelf.

Mitchell couldn't help himself but intently watch the flesh revealed by her low-cut top bounce as she mixed liquids in a cocktail shaker. He lifted his eyes to meet hers as she passed a glass over the bar. Fog danced on the surface of the liquid that glowed green beneath the lights.

He threw a bit of the drink to the back of his throat, his facing contorting in protest at the taste that burned his tongue. He shook off a shiver that overtook him with the strength of the alcohol before he looked back to Marissa's face. "So," he said. "Got any leads for me?"

She sighed. "Well," she said, pointing with her finger toward the crowd. "That one seems like she's trouble. The slutty kind of trouble—*your* kind of trouble. Try your luck there."

"That one?" He turned, leaning his back against the bar with the support of his elbows on it, and nodded toward a woman dancing alone. Her straight blonde hair fell just below her exposed shoulders. A tube top stretched to its limit over her large breasts. Jeans hugged her legs from beneath black leather boots and met her exposed belly at her hips.

"Yep. That one." Marissa finally turned away to tend to other patrons awaiting their service.

Mitchell drained the glass and set it on the bar before he began walking toward the woman. He could feel the agony beginning to swell behind the zipper of his pants, and his mouth watered with the hope of satiation.

Leaning against the wall near the girl, watching her, he waited for the smile that he was sure would arrive. It did. "Hi," he said cheerfully, returning the expression. "I haven't seen you here before." He cringed internally at the cheesy line.

The girl continued her gentle bouncing to the rhythm of the bass and saw-wave synthesizer that permeated from the speakers. She allowed a sort of chuckle to escape her lips before she replied. "I'm just barhopping," she said, her voice raised above the music. "Never heard of this place before. Figured I'd give it a try."

"Alone?" He leaned closer to the girl so that she could hear his words, catching the floral scent that radiated from her skin and hair. He inhaled deeply to savor it.

"No," the girl replied. She squinted her eyes and scanned the crowd. "I'm not sure where my friends went." She shrugged. "They're always sort of ditching me when we're out."

"Ah," Mitchell said, raising his eyebrows for a second. "I was going to say, there are a lot of weirdos that come here. If you're alone, maybe I should stick around with you to keep you safe."

She laughed, her gleaming eyes scanning Mitchell. "You're cute," she said.

"Oh, thank you," replied Mitchell. "You're not so bad yourself."

"No." She shook her head with a smile. "I mean your shitty attempts at flirting with me. I can basically feel the desperation coming off of you."

Mitchell felt a wash of heat crawl up his face, and his eyes slipped their focus to the floor.

The girl allowed a wordless moment to pass between them. "What's your name?" she finally asked.

"Mitchell Townsend," he replied sheepishly. "You?"

"Clara," the girl replied. She turned her whole body to face him and placed her hand gently on the back of his neck, running her fingernails into his freshly cut hair. "Look, Mitchell, it's okay. I like that you had the balls to even come over here and talk to me. The rest of these pussies haven't given me anything but a stare-down from across the room. Besides, you're kind of hot, and that makes up for what you lack in flirtation." She fluttered her eyes a bit and moved her body closer to his.

"Well, I—" Mitchell's words were cut off when she pulled his head closer to her face and planted a firm kiss on his mouth, gently grazing her teeth against his bottom lip.

She pulled her face away from his. The rhythm of his pounding heart in his ears was almost enough to drown out the music. He looked over her again and noticed he'd placed his hands in the dips of her waist.

"Come on." She nodded her head toward the door. "I haven't had much luck at all tonight until you came along." She gently gripped his hand, and he waded through the crowd behind her at her direction.

"What about your friends?" Mitchell called to Clara as she opened the door to the street. He almost wanted to kick himself for a question that may have strayed the focus from what was sure to happen now, or worse yet, allow the girl to reconsider abandoning her friends for sex with a stranger.

Clara didn't reply until they reached the quiet of the sidewalk, where the sound from behind the door seemed distant and muffled. "Oh," she said. "I'm sure they'll meet up with us at some point." She bit her lower lip. "But I'll make sure it's not until I am finished with you."

⎯◆◇◆⎯

THE CAR MITCHELL CALLED finally pulled up to the curb. He approached the vehicle and opened the door for Clara, receiving an excited giggle in return for his gesture. He slid next to her on the leather of the back seat and shut the door.

"Where to?" the driver said with a smile.

Clara looked over at Mitchell with curious eyes. "My place or yours?" she asked.

"Well," Mitchell said. "We can't go to my place." He chuckled nervously.

"Why?" she replied, nudging him playfully. "You *married* or something?"

"I..." Mitchell began. He took a moment to dig around in his mind for a convincing explanation.

"It's okay," she replied, cutting off his mental probing. "I honestly don't care." An almost sinister but enticing smile filled her expression. "All the better. I kind of like the idea of stealing another woman's man."

Mitchell let a small sigh of relief escape. His night wouldn't be ruined after all.

"You two got that figured out?" the driver said, looking into the rear-view mirror. He tapped the GPS on the dashboard with his finger.

"We'll go to my motel room," Clara quickly replied. She rattled off the address, and the driver's fingers followed swiftly on the touch screen. The driver put the car in gear, and the engine picked up as they headed toward their destination.

Clara slid her slender fingers upward along Mitchell's thigh with one hand, while the other found the back of his neck. She pulled his head forward to lock her mouth to his in with fiery lust. The driver made a noise when he noticed the activity behind him, but Mitchell ignored it in favor of the welling desire that bubbled inside of him, and the thought that this had been all too easy to achieve.

⸻◆⸻

THE CAR SLOWED TO a stop with a gentle squeal of worn brakes. Mitchell peered out the window to a parking lot devoid of parked cars. The expanse of pavement was slightly illuminated by flickering, pink lights on a sign situated above the reception office, its windows dark in their after hours. He opened the car door.

Trying to ignore an emergent uneasy feeling, he outstretched his hand to gently grasp Clara's. She stood on the pavement and shut the door behind her. Mitchell watched as the car made a left turn onto the road and drove away. He was now completely alone with the girl.

"Come on," said Clara, guiding Mitchell along a line of doors until she stopped at one of them. She produced a key card from her purse and bent over slightly, pressing her ass against the crotch of Mitchell's jeans as she slid the key into the hole for the deadbolt. She unlocked the door, opened it, and permitted him inside with a gesture.

Flicking a switch along the wall, Clara sparked the lights, which revealed a standard and cheap motel room. Against one of the dirty walls, which he guessed were once white, was a bed with maroon pillows and a blanket of the same hue. Dingy nightstands stood on either side of the bed. Against the wall across from the foot of the bed stood a dresser with four drawers that housed a cheap, boxy television. In the corner, near a sliding glass door that led onto a back porch, was a small desk with a chair.

"It's not much," said Clara as she placed her purse on the nightstand. "But it's an affordable, comfortable place to stay while I'm here."

"Are you from out of town?" Mitchell inquired.

Clara simply shrugged. "Sort of. I'm from Massachusetts," she said with a wave of her hand. "Are you here to interview me, or are you here to fuck me?" She raised an eyebrow and squinted her eyes at Mitchell, a beckoning expression. She slipped the tube top off, her tits bouncing with their release.

His mouth began to water at the sight of her nipples, already hard atop their pink mounds of firm flesh. He stood almost frozen in his stare at a sight that was better than what he had even imagined.

She approached him with a slow and graceful sway. "What?" she said softly. "Are you afraid?" She stripped him of his shirt and gently ran her hands down his chest.

He bit his lip and swallowed hard before placing his mouth on the curve where her neck met her shoulder. He inhaled her scent and gently bit at her skin, savoring the soft moan that whispered past her lips at his touch.

Taking him by the hand, she fell to her back on the bed and pulled him on top of her. He firmly ran his hands along her shape until he reached the denim of her jeans that clung tightly to her hips. Finding the button, he unfastened it and slid the zipper down. He tore them down the length of her smooth legs with fervent animal lust.

With eyes closed and mouths locked, he felt Clara's hand tug open his belt and pull upon the zipper of his jeans. Her warm hand quickly dove into his boxers to retrieve his now throbbing dick. She gently ran her hands along the shaft before guiding it between her legs to run the tip along the warm and abundant fluids in her slit.

He plunged with the thrust of his hips. She pressed her body against him with an arch of her back. He pumped with the rhythm of her rolling hips, drowning in her ecstasy. He firmly gripped a bouncing tit, and she dug into his back with her fingernails.

He gripped harder. He pounded with primal need. His face twisted with the welcomed agony of orgasm. Forcing a bestial groan from the depths of his throat, he dumped his fluid deep inside her.

He collapsed on top of the girl, catching his breath before he rolled off to lie beside her. As the embers of passion cooled, the icy winds of guilt pricked him. They always did. His mind turned to the image of his wife, sitting on the sofa in their living room alone with the television flashing light on her sad face. Dread burrowed deeply into the pit of his stomach.

It wasn't that his continual betrayal was something that he necessarily wanted, it was that his compulsion left him no other choice. There was no satiation without constant sacrifices to the monster that lived inside him. And the more he fed it, the more it wanted. He became emptier and emptier for it.

Pushing himself to sit upright, he quietly pulled his jeans back up and refastened his zipper, button, and belt. His hand then retrieved the cell phone from his pocket and thumbed the passcode into the touch screen.

Clara gave him an inquisitive expression. "Where are you going?"

He sighed. "I'm going to call a ride home." He could feel the remorse in his voice. "I should really get back to my wife."

"Aw, no." She forced her bottom lip out in mock sadness. "Can't you just stay with me a little longer?" She playfully patted the mattress with her hand. "Who knows? Maybe there's a round two ahead of you in your night with me. That's probably more than your wife ever gives you."

"I don't know."

"Come on. At least let me give you a back rub before you go?"

Mitchell remained silent for a few moments, mulling the offer over. He studied the girl, her breasts still exposed, skin tightly wrapped around her perfect hourglass figure. Conflict raged in his stomach. "Alright," he said, finally. "A back rub, and then I *have* to go." He lay on his stomach, burying his face into his arms that were crossed along the pillow.

"Let me just get some lotion," Clara said as she began to dig through the contents of her purse. "Okay," she said after a moment.

Mitchell could feel her still-slippery warmth against his lower back as she straddled him. The tips of her fingers dug deep into the tissues in his back, and he let a quiet groan slip as he began to relax. The sensations melted his dread, and he loosened his tense shoulders against the now fading wishes to just get up and leave.

His mind had begun to slip into the comfort of sleep when he felt Clara's hand firmly grasp the back of his neck. Quickly after her fingers squeezed, there was a painful pinch in the side of his neck, and a powerfully cold sensation spread outward into his body. He threw the girl off his back and looked at her with a growing sense of rage. "What the fuck?"

Clara stood at the side of the bed, and she laughed. He spotted an empty syringe with a long, thick needle in her hand.

He uselessly squirmed. His limbs felt glued to the mattress, too heavy to lift. His vision began to blur. Overwhelming nausea swept across his head, leaving the room spinning around him. "What did you..." His voice began to fade.

Leaning in to give him a soft kiss on his forehead, Clara moved her mouth to his ear. She whispered in some strange language. The alien syllables and sounds became a phantom hand that reached into his skull and scratched at his brain. Then, the unconscious dark took him.

⸺◆⸺

MITCHELL OPENED HIS EYES and blinked against the groggy sleep that lingered. Cold concrete touched the skin of his exposed upper body. He shivered against it before he sat himself upright with a quiet, echoing grunt. He rubbed away a blur that held on to his vision, and he studied the room he was in.

Directly across from where he sat was a windowless metal door that promised a struggle to open—if it wasn't locked, of course. Around that, to meet at four corners, was stained and aged concrete. A single bulb hung from the ceiling to provide a dim, yellow light that almost failed to quell the shadows in the corners.

Standing, Mitchell dusted the denim of his jeans with his hands. He checked his pockets to find his belongings missing—his cell phone filled with contacts he could call for help and his wallet that housed his credit cards and driver's license where his home address was printed—before he reached around to feel his where it had been stabbed. It was tender, and he sucked a bit of air through his teeth with a wince. He checked his fingers for any sign of blood, but it seemed the small wound had been long dried.

He squinted and turned to scan the room again. His focus fell to a notebook lying in the far corner behind where he stood. He slowly approached it, fighting the weakness that still faded in his legs. He crouched to pick it up and moved to sit directly beneath the light in the center.

The corners and edges of the pages showed signs of decay, and the paper itself was brittle and marked with dried stains of deep greens and browns. The words scrawled across the paper were mostly illegible; the letters distorted where wetness from another time had been heavy enough to spread the ink around. There were, however, a few words that could be read, and some were entirely unmarred throughout—he could see the name Osborne sprinkled about, and could gather something about hills, woodlands, and a farmhouse. One unknown word irked him. He squinted at it, perplexed. "*Shoggoth*," he read aloud in a whisper to himself. He hadn't seen it anywhere before.

He continued flipping through the pages, beyond where the writing suddenly stopped mid-sentence. After a few pages that only housed blue lines, there was more. Some scribbles from an obviously different hand wrote about finding *it*, whatever that may have meant—but it seemed as though whatever was found was something important, judging by the frantic appearance of the letters. Perhaps the notebook itself? He mused. Further, more words were written about a gate remaining open. The scribblings of some crazy person, he concluded.

He fingered through another few pages until even fresher ink was found. Large letters overtook the entire piece of paper, and the lines appeared to be quickly scratched, as if a shaky, nervous hand had written them. It was a sort of poem, which read:

Descend, descend, descend,
To a place as cold and quiet
As the walk of Ithaqua winds,
And hands will search,
Where no eyes can see.
Soon within your grasp will be,
The initial steps to obtaining the key.

Mitchell sat in thought for long, passing moment in the silence. Maybe the notebook was left for a purpose—maybe it was intended that he read it and find the poetry, so he'd explore its meaning. He wondered about the key. A tool to find for his escape? This could be some sick game for the amusement of his captors. But, he fought off the thought, considering then that his blurry head was connecting the writings of this room's previous prisoner to his own current captivity.

Prisoner, he thought. He jumped to his feet. Images raced across his inner vision of his murder. He wondered how long they would wait before they would come for him. Did they mean to torture him a while, playing with his agony, before they got bored and ended his life? His face contorted with the desperate wish to be at home with his wife. He ran his hand down the length of his face.

Anxiety rushed through him like fire. A frantic urge to scrape his fingernails against the floor to dig a way out overtook him. He looked at the door, and he rushed toward it. Shaky fingers found its handle. Muscles flexed with desperation to pull it inward. With a harsh scrape, it opened. *Unlocked.*

He escaped into a long corridor lined with metal doors set into the same cement walls, where flickering tubes of dirty fluorescent lights traced the center of the ceiling high above his head. He quickly visited the doors as he made his way along the narrow hall, pushing or pounding upon them to no avail.

Finally, an ear-piercing screech resounded against his surroundings as a door gave way. Behind it was a stairwell that descended to a landing. It was lit by a bulb that hung from a wire, dimly illuminating a set of double doors. He hesitated before he began his descent.

A thick chain tied the handles together. A large padlock made of thick metal hung from the chain. He pushed against the door to see how far they'd open. There was a small bit of give that allowed a razor thin beam of light to infect the darkness around him. *The light of day*, his mind screamed at him. He forced himself against the metal harder, slamming his shoulder against it until it had become numb. He forced his throat raw from screaming through the small crack for help that would probably never hear him.

He stepped back from the door, breathless and having given up. He noticed a word carved into the wood. *Down*, it said simply. Next to it, an arrow was carved, pointing downward to the left. He turned to the next flight of stairs, longer and held in darker shadow. He began his slow descent.

At the stairs' end, he found a narrow hallway. A few inches of water hugged his ankles as he stepped into its length. He trudged forward, the splashing smacking against the quiet around him. A fluorescent tube in the ceiling popped ahead, showering sparks downward and causing his heart to palpitate as he cowered for a moment.

A dark room waited for him ahead. He entered. A sudden and severe coldness clawed his skin. It was wide and shadowy to his left, and another bulb hung from the ceiling in a far corner. A dark green substance floated, lightly brushing his ankles as it moved gently along the surface of the water. It was thick and icier than the air.

A dripping sound echoed in the quiet. Distant and from a darker area of the basement expansion. He flashed his eyes toward the area of the noise as he moved slowly toward the light.

On the walls on either side of the corner, written from what looked like the same substance that floated in the water, were words. The wet letters trickled down the concrete before they dried. On one wall, it read:

You did nothing to stop it. Not with her, not with anyone. You are perfect for The Mother.

Scribbled on the other, another poem:

Through the hole
Along the wall
Within, a stone
For Mother of All.
When hands do find
Upon the floor,
Take it to top,
In three of door
You'll see inside
A figure who stands
As pale as mask
Of Unspeakable Hastur.

Beneath the poem, an arrow that pointed toward the almost material darkness. Mitchell placed his hands against the cold cement and moved toward where the dripping seemed now grew in pace. His eyes eventually became blind and useless, so he closed them and continued to feel until his fingers found a crevice that widened to an opening a few feet above the watery floor. He would have to crawl through.

Inside, a pervasive smell of rot invaded his nostrils. The dripping sounds grew in volume. He felt the cramped space open above him, and he tumbled into the floor below with another crawl forward. He regained his bearings and got back to his hands and knees to slosh around in the water. His fingered tingled with numbness from the cold as he searched for the stone mentioned in the poem on the wall. His body convulsed with uncontrollable shivering.

"Come on," he whispered. "Where the fuck are you?"

Something shuffled near him. He snapped his head upward and listened. Something *heard* him.

He searched and crawled and sloshed harder.

There it was. Flat against the ground and completely submerged was a stone with smooth, round edges. He traced its surface and felt etchings on its surface. He lifted it from the floor. A sudden guttural droning responded to his action. It was loud and like a cacophony of croaking frogs mixed with the sound of throat singing. Splashing and slurping met the droning, like something wet and sticky rubbing against itself.

Mitchell crouched, frozen with terror. He kept his eyes closed tight against the dark.

The splashing of what could have been many sets of legs pushed the dirty water around. The pool ebbed and flowed in waves against his skin. The droning began to slowly draw out the enunciation of words in a mockery of human speech. *Eeeeeuhhhh shub nigguraaaaaath,* it throated, loud, deep, and monotone. The voice caressed his body with vibration.

His muscles tensed. His legs wanted to spring to propel him away, but he wasn't sure in which direction he faced. He had to make a decision quickly. The splash of water against him became stronger. The voice became louder. Whatever was in this room with him moved toward him.

He turned completely around. He clutched the stone tighter. And he crawled forward until his head made contact with the wall. Placing his hand against the vertical concrete, he inched himself along until he found the hole he had got in here from. Or, he hoped against hope that it was the same hole and not one that'd lead him somewhere deeper into this hell. He crawled through, scraping his stomach along the tunnel's floor.

He reached the other side, and his eyelids detected light. He opened his eyes and squinted. He found himself in a tight area with only a few feet between the wall behind him and that which was in front of him. On either side of him were more long and narrow hallways. The electric buzz of struggling lights filled the otherwise silent air.

He stood for a few moments, allowing the relative warmth of the air—at least compared to the place from which he just came—to burn off what lingering shivers it could considering the cold wet of his skin and pants. He rubbed his free hand against his arm before the other lifted the stone. It wasn't exceptionally large, and it was surprisingly lightweight. He looked at the etchings on the surface, tracing his finger along them.

There were two sharp lines that ran parallel to one another along the outer edge. They both formed a hexagonal border. Within the lines of the hexagon were what looked to be words written in symbols of some language he had never seen. Inside the confines of the border were a series of sigils carved in a pattern. A light headache gripped his forehead, and his thoughts began to fragment with his gazing at the symbol. He shifted his eyes away and rubbed his face.

Drawing a deep breath and forcing it from his lungs, he turned to take the corridor to his left.

—◆○◆—

HE WANDERED FOR HOURS. He followed the paths of hallways where corners would turn to meet a wall. He found doors which led to upward staircases that only peaked to another set that went back down. Other times, he had found himself following a corridor that led him directly back to where he started. He'd yet to find the *top* and *three of door* that he had been searching for.

Lost and utterly exhausted, Mitchell pressed his back against the wall, sliding down and slumping with a sigh. He wondered whether he would find this key and be able to escape. He wondered if he would ever see his wife again. Closing his eyes, he visualized her face. "Elizabeth," he whispered into the dim quiet. "I miss you. I'm sorry." The wetness of tears stained the stubble on his cheeks.

Something whispered back. The words themselves were unclear, but it was *something*.

He forced himself to his feet, intending to follow whatever replied. He staggered forward with the stone in one hand and the other using a wall for support. "Elizabeth?" He called, his delirium considering the possibility. His outcry reverberated, the emotion in his voice echoing back to him.

The whispering continued. It grew into louder, multiple voices. His pace quickened as he continued his trailing of the sound. He charged forward into the shadows that lie around a corner, but was stopped by a large metal door. He felt its surface in search of the handle until he found it. He twisted his wrist and pulled to open it.

The other side revealed another long stairwell that ascended beyond where his eyes could follow it. An ambient squirming darted across his hearing as he began to climb, as if something crawled away. He saw nothing that could have made the sound.

The top of the stairs yielded another door. He waited before pushing against it. The room across its threshold held three doors. *The top*, he thought to himself with relief. *Three of door.*

He tried, first, to open the door on the right. It seemed jammed or locked and would not budge, and the middle was the same. He pulled the final door. It opened with the loud squeal of old, protesting hinges.

In the center of the room, the nude hourglass figure of a pale woman stood upright with its legs crossed. Her face had a mouth with thin lips and a slender nose, but only porcelain flesh stretched over the eye sockets of the skull beneath it. Her arms were cradled in front of her, the curl of her fingers suggested a desire to hold something. A small wooden table stood next to the figure, housing a simple golden chalice.

He approached the figure, noticing the shallow rise and fall of her breasts. She twitched as if she noticed him, and she let out a soft moan. She then tilted her head forward, as if focusing on the stone that he carried. He placed it in her hands, and her fingers, one-by-one, gripped its edges.

She uncrossed and spread her legs, lowering to a squat with shuddering motion.

He stepped back and noticed the blue-tinged labia that dangled from beneath the mound between her legs. She tilted her head back and shifted with a struggle to turn toward the table. She opened her mouth wide.

Mitchell grabbed the chalice from the table. "Is this what you want?"

The woman sighed with ecstasy.

He looked inside and saw the chalice contained a thick, white fluid. A moldy, putrid odor emanated from it, and he jerked his head away from the cup's mouth. He slowly poured the liquid into the woman's mouth.

She began convulsing. Her chest rose and fell with deeper breaths. Her mouth opened wide to shout orgasmic elations. Black splotches formed on her skin, webbing outward to overtake her flesh. Small tentacles emerged from her throat, born to writhe in ecstatic pleasure. They wrapped her face and reached to touch her neck. Mitchell thought she might collapse.

Wet, slapping noises echoed. He followed the sound to find dark green and black sludge being expelled from the woman's vaginal orifice. The substance stained the white of her thighs and calves as it splashed on impact. Something glimmered silver within the sludge: *a key.*

He crouched and plunged his fingers into the filth. He grabbed the key, and he ran back to the door through which he entered this room. As he swung it open, her moans grew louder from pleasure and pain.

———◈———

Mitchell finally found his way back to the double doors that gave him a hint of the outside world. He fumbled with the lock on the chains. He inserted the key with trembling hands. And he disengaged the lock.

His thoughts swam with the idea of finding a way home—he didn't care how. He just wanted to wrap himself beneath the blankets of his bed, next to the comforting warmth of his wife. He promised himself that his marital betrayals would stop, whatever it took. He'd cover this part of his life beneath even more carefully thought alibis, and he'd move on with his new-found faithful existence. Hell, he'd go to therapy.

He tore the chains free from the handles with vigor. The chains fell to the floor with a chorus of metallic clangs.

He opened the doors, and night bathed him in its darkness. He stepped onto a dirt road that led into a forest ahead. He ran against his exhaustion, his panging, excruciating hunger. He ran against the cold that still clung to his skin.

The forest ahead swallowed him. The trees whispered as the breeze rustled their leaves. The sound of his stomping feet mingled with the cries of nocturnal animals. And then it mingled with the rhythm of distant, heavy drumming. He slowed his pace and listened.

He noticed the glow of fires ahead, bathing the leaves in orange light. He heard chanting and wailing. The drums grew louder and faster.

He hid in the brush on the side of the path and reconsidered his plan of escape. He watched the dancing light and listened. He could run through woods to safety. The sound of the gathering ahead would cover sticks that snapped and leaves that crunched beneath his feet.

He stood and turned. He ran. Branches smacked him across his face with his flight, but he didn't care.

He made it back to the edge of the woods. He was met with four robed figures dressed in cowled black robes. They saw him and approached. The center two figures had obvious female features pushing against the cloth of their robes.

Clara and Marissa.

"No!" he screamed with a force that pained his chest. He dropped to his knees with tears welling in his eyes, digging his fingers into the dirt. "No," he repeated, softer this time.

"Congratulations, Mitchell," Clara said, a smile crawling into her cheeks. "You solved the puzzles, recovered the talisman. Everything." She extended her arms at her sides. "And here I didn't think you were so clever."

"Fuck you," Mitchell spat with venom. His scowl wanted to sear the flesh upon her face.

Marissa giggled with condescension.

Clara shook her head with a smug expression. "Now, now," she said, her voice glazed with the tone of condescension. "Is that how you treat somebody who brought you a special gift?"

Mitchell scowled more deeply. "What are you talking about?" he asked fiercely. "What is this?" He gestured toward the path. "And what was all that shit in there?" He threw his arm behind him to point at the building.

"Come," replied Clara with a beckoning motion of her hand. "And we will show you."

He watched as Clara and Marissa began to walk away, but the men that flanked her remained. "I'm not going anywhere with you freaks."

Clara stopped, turning her head. "Yes, you are," she replied, nodding at the two men.

He tried to fight them as they tucked their arms beneath his and lifted him upright, but his waning strength permitted them victory. Mitchell's heels dragged through the dirt as they moved him forward toward the forest. The congregation followed behind.

They dragged Mitchell along the path. The silhouetted mess of trees and plants swayed with the violent build of wind blended into the darkness of storm clouds that gathered angrily above. A roar of thunder gave way with a power that shook the ground. Rain began to pelt his face.

They came into a small group of nude adherents dancing and prancing around a large bonfire in front of a stone altar. Their shadows moved against the woods like monsters. A pungent odor of rot and soured body fluids built along their slow journey into the congregation, and the sudden humidity strengthened the scents.

Clara and Marissa stopped again. The men that dragged him threw him to the ground, and then forced him to his knees toward the perverse dance of worship. The heat of the bonfire bathed his skin, and he was almost thankful for it.

He tilted his head toward the ground. One man grabbed his hair and ripped at his scalp, forcing him to watch.

Something danced beyond the shadows of the trees to the rhythm of the thunderous drumming that the congregation now produced. It approached with a deep droning that mixed with the sounds of the worshipers. It was the same set of sounds that Mitchell heard in that dark room where he found that stone that he could now see resting on the level stone of the altar. But it called with a deeper throat, thunderous and horrible. A goliath noise that human ears should never be subjected to. The somethings kept coming and coming, a looming, darker shadow against the storm that raged above.

And they emerged from the sea of illuminated trees. Creatures whose height reached beyond the canopy of the forest, made of ropy black, slithering tentacles that ended in a multitude of drooling mouths hungrily grinding and snapping razor teeth. Eyes blinked along the length of their tentacles in chaotic patterns, and they rolled about in all directions as if searching for prey. They slowly moved, walking on a cluster of thick, black-haired legs that ended at hooves. Their shapes constantly shifted as they trudged.

Mitchell breathed heavily through his teeth that clenched with pain and watched. The creatures bowed and placed some of their mouths against the ground in what looked like prayer. He wanted to squirm at the sound of their guttural chanting.

The noise of the crowd dulled a bit, but it did not stop, as Clara commanded attention from the position she took at the stone altar. Amid the now softer but still deep and rhythmic drumming, and amid the thunder and rasped chanting of the creatures, she began to shout. "Tonight," she said, raising her arms above her head. One hand firmly gripped the black handle of a dagger with a wide blade. "From the court of Azathoth at the center of our vast and indifferent universe, from the depths of the realm of Yaddith, we shall evoke our great and perverse mother!"

The crowd replied to her in unintelligible cries. They threw their hands into the air with vigorous passion.

"Tonight," Clara continued. She lowered her hands, extending them outward as if to feel the electric charge of the air. She raised her head to peer at the sky for a moment before she lowered it again to make eye contact with Mitchell. A sinister grin appeared. "We bring her gifts."

Mitchell could feel beads of sweat trickle down his shirtless back. His heart pounded in his ears. He realized suicide would have been the better option in that building than the decisions he had made to follow the scavenger hunt that led to his own murder.

"Bring the sacrifice!" Clara screamed with a rasp, throwing her arms wide. Her face was alight with a wide and hungry smile.

A rush of fear ate his insides. He prepared himself to be led to the altar. But the men who held him in place made no move to take him there. He watched as a few from the gathering went into the woods.

They returned with a woman. Her long, dark and disheveled hair framed her terrified face, twisted into sobs and smeared with black makeup. She was nude, with her hands bound behind her back. Her body trembled. She begged and screamed.

Anger burned Mitchell's insides. Adrenaline coursed through his body. He forced himself free from the hands that gripped his arm. *"Elizabeth!"* he screamed with a burning throat against the thunder, the drumming, and the chanting. Baring his teeth with something that was deeper than rage, he began charging toward the altar. His eyes caught the pleading gaze of his wife. She recognized him with wide eyes.

The blunt force of a fist made contact with the back of his head, forcing him back to the ground. He saw stars and fell back to the ground.

He lifted his head to see that Clara had forced Elizabeth to bend at the hips with her head directly above the flat stone. She gripped a handful of Elizabeth's hair, and she ripped her head upward to face the gathering.

Mitchell whispered his wife's name and locked his eyes locked to hers. The sound echoed in his own mind above the howling and shouting. And he watched the blood pour on the talisman as Clara slid the knife across Elizabeth's throat. She convulsed, choking.

He gasped. A weakness overcame his limbs, and he fell with a tremble to the mud that sucked at his body. His widened eyes looked as if they could see the hope dissipate into the air. His despair burned away any concern that may have been left for his own well-being.

The cackling and howling from the mouths of the congregants stabbed at his ears. The droning of the monsters grew with intensity. And then the noises dulled again.

Mitchell peered with hate at the altar ahead. Clara stood with her hand still full of Elizabeth's hair. Her limp and lifeless body hung above the altar. Her dead eyes still looked in Mitchell's direction.

Clara raised the bloody dagger toward the sky. Her eyes glazed over. "Ia! Shub-Niggurath!" she shouted with a force that shot globs of saliva from her tongue.

The crowd returned her exclamation in ecstatic unison. The tentacles of the nightmare creatures stretched upward and shook, and they, too, droned the same phrase.

A deep, buzzing whir rumbled to outmatch the thunder that growled above. Trees snapped and fell in the near distance. Something else approached. Bigger. Horrific. Something more horrible than what came from those trees before. It had to have been. Mitchell wanted to close his eyes, but they remained fixed on the direction from where the sounds emanated.

A mass of black blanketed the sky. It seemed to quell even the light of the bonfires. The gargantuan, hunching abomination swept the air with massive tentacles that protruded from its undulating form. He felt the heat of its repugnant breath as its many mouths opened wide with yellow, cracked, and knife-edged teeth to release a cry that he thought might shatter his eardrums.

In the presence of the beast, beneath its thick, almost tangible shadow, the congregation broke out into orgiastic indulgences, except for Clara. Alone in her exclusion from the squirming mess of group copulation, she approached him where he knelt.

He lifted his scowl toward her.

"You should be more grateful, you know," she said, raising her voice above the moaning and laughing that mixed with the monstrous sounds. A smirk crawled across her expression.

The words fueled the searing fire of hatred within Mitchell. He said nothing. He just stared, wishing he could murder this woman.

"You've been chosen by the Mother."

Mitchell shook his head. He didn't know what to make of her words, and he didn't really care what she meant. "What?" he said. "I don't even know what any of this bullshit is. I don't even—"

"Yes, you do. You always have worshipped her, even if unaware. Your lust has always driven you, and it's now led you here, to where you were always meant to be." She allowed a sigh to slip and smiled gently. "To an honor greater than any of us here have ever been rewarded with, despite our relentless devotion." Her eyes narrowed and locked on Mitchell's. "Gof'nn hupadgh Shub-Niggurath," she hissed before she walked away.

A tentacled reached from behind Clara. Mitchell opened his eyes wide with terror. He felt its tight grip wrap around his body. The slime that coated the appendage burned his skin. The monster lifted him. His feet dangled above the ground, and it pulled him toward its mass of squirming goatish legs that widened to reveal a gaping orifice that secreted a substance of green, black, and brown.

Miniature caricatures of the tentacles of its greater form writhed from inside the puckering, flexing hole that breathed a putrid stink. They replaced the hold of the larger tentacle. He turned his head with disgust as he was pulled inward to the sucking hole to be devoured.

The creature squeezed Mitchell with its pulsing, slick vaginal walls. The heavy, hot humidity coupled with the stench stole his conscious mind.

—◦—

WEEKS HAD PASSED SINCE he opened his eyes to the light of the sun in a body he did not know, slathered in the filthy wet after he guessed he had been spat back out. He had looked at his new legs: inversely jointed and covered in stringy black hairs. He felt the bulges at his brow, and other hideous transformations that left his face more animal than man.

He was overcome with an inextinguishable, agonizing lust that cramped the muscles of his thighs with an unimaginable hunger. This new drive—this new *need* to hunt for sexual prey—rivaled even that of his previous life.

He could remember who he was—he remembered that he was once Mitchell Townsend, husband of Elizabeth Townsend. He was able to recall the sweet sound of laughter and the warmth beneath the blanket as he and Elizabeth huddled together on the couch to joke, to watch movies, to make love. The images were clearer than they had ever been, and his regret was a deep running river that carved canyons of pain. He wanted to tear into the pit of his stomach with the sharp claws that now sat at the ends of his fingers.

The satyr looked over the expanse beyond the edge of the cliff where he stood. He watched as the sun began to dip itself beyond the horizon of the vast forest. Sucking air between his sharp teeth, he crouched and then lunged himself over the edge. The plunge was far, but the fall was quick. His body smashed against the rocky ground with a crunch of bones.

Despite the sudden stop of the fall, he did not die—he *could not* die, having been gifted with some undesired immortality. So, he lay there beneath the dusk, alone with his thoughts. He mouthed a phrase that seemed to be summoned of its own will, "Ia, Shub-Niggurath." His breath whispered the phrase into the wind that carried it.

5

CORNELIA

BRENNAN CONTINUED THE UPHILL walk while cursing whoever decided this winding country road didn't need streetlights. Snow filled his shoes more and more with each step forward. He watched fog dance from his mouth with a sigh.

He was thankful for the guardrail that separated him from the ravine. He probably wouldn't have been able to tell where the buried pavement ended without it. He'd drank enough alcohol at the dive bar a few miles back to be wearing a whiskey jacket that he thought could keep a polar bear warm. And Justin was even drunker than he was, so he'd have been no help.

Hell, he'd have probably died down the hill before him anyway, with the way he was stumbling.

"You think there are bears around?" Brennan asked Justin, his drunken mind shifting the conversation.

Justin laughed. "Probably, man. Bears might be the least of our worries, though. Pennsylvania woods are home to all kinds of freakish shit."

"If a bear came out of those woods, like, right now." He pointed a finger toward the snow-laden trees. "It would eat your ass first."

"Why's that?"

"Gingers have a little more spice to them."

A snowball collided with the back of Brennan's head. He turned his head to shout behind him. "You fucker!"

Justin laughed.

Brennan walked into the middle of the road. He almost slipped where the snow had been packed by tires. He spread his arms wide and yelled into the darkness that swallowed the bend ahead. "Come at me, you shits! Give me what you got!"

Only the echo of his voice answered him.

He turned around to face Justin, walking backward.

A light swelled from around the corner behind him. The snow glistened. His shadow danced with the shadows of the trees along the white surface.

He turned. A car came around the bend. The driver must have lost control on the ice. The car was sideways, sliding fast. Faster than he could move.

He tried.

Justin cried for him to get out of the road.

The car collided with him. He felt his body push into the door. Then he felt himself being dragged along the snow and ice.

"Oh, *shit*," his friend yelled.

But the voice faded. So did the view of the falling snow.

⸻◄○►⸻

BRENNAN'S EYES SNAPPED OPEN. He gasped. He tried to catch his breath. He felt his body and realized he was naked besides still wearing a pair of boxers. And he was lying in an unfamiliar bed.

He didn't realize how badly his head hurt until he fought against the tight muscles in his neck to turn it. So, he straightened his neck and allowed his head to sink back into the pillow.

Cracks crawled across the white ceiling above him. A ceiling fan sat dormant at the center of the room. It looked as if one blade had rotted and broken off at its middle at some point. Layers of dust collected on that and the remaining blades. He guessed the condition came from years of neglect.

The room, from what he could see of it from lying here like this, seemed empty. He could see a nightstand in his peripheral vision. A lamp with a tilted, yellow-stained lampshade, which looked to be another home for dust, stood on the nightstand's surface.

One blind-less, shadeless window indented the papered walls. The snow-reflected sunlight that beamed through the smeared glass intensified his headache. Nausea swirled in his stomach. He squinted and shifted his eyes and swallowed against the urge to puke.

The night before flooded back into his memory. He remembered headlights and fear, and the smell of the crisp winter air before everything went blank.

He wondered if Justin dragged him off the road and brought him to an abandoned house so he could call for help in the morning when the roads were cleared. But the sheets under him seemed clean. So did the comforter that covered his legs and the pillowcase. He knew his friend didn't have a bed set in his jacket.

He slowly, carefully pushed himself into a sitting position, resting his back against the wall at the head of the mattress. His head swam with pain and dizziness, which was probably a combination of a hangover and the damage he took from getting hit by that car.

He winced when he tried to bend his legs upward and decided not to fight against the pain in his knees.

He could see the floor now. What looked like old newspaper clipping spread scattered across the floor. Some of them collected in piles near corners and in random places with no apparent planning. He couldn't make out what was printed on them. Some of the ink had long faded, and some papers were torn from being stepped on.

The window held a view of nothing but trees. Snow weighed down their skeletal branches. The woods stretched far and deep. He hoped the other side of this house was connected to the road and wasn't too remote. He needed help.

The door opened with a creak. He turned his head to look.

A woman walked in. She carefully carried a tray that had a bowl and a cup on it. "Oh, you're awake," she said. She smiled and blew a strand of blonde hair away from her face. Her clothes hung loose on her: a baggy black sweatshirt and an olive jacket that looked like it had been worn by a soldier before she got hold of it. Her denim jeans swished as she walked further into the room. "I was starting to get a little worried." She gently set the tray on Brennan's lap.

Brennan sipped from the glass of water without thinking. He cleared his throat and set it back on the tray. The bowl contained some kind of meat and vegetable soup. He could feel the heat when the steam rose to his face. The aroma was almost intoxicating.

The woman chuckled. "It's okay." She must have noticed his uncertainty. "I know you don't know me. Eat and drink if you want; if not, I won't be offended. I just think it's important for you to get your strength back."

He played with the spoon for a second. "Thank you."

"Of course."

He looked up from the bowl. "Is my friend here? Justin? He was with me when I got hit last night."

Her eyes shifted back-and-forth. "You were alone when we found you lying on the road. I'm sorry to say that I don't know who your friend is." Then she smiled again. "Maybe he went to get help or something. I'm sure he'll be happy to reconnect once you're doing better."

We? Anxiety gnawed on his insides for a second. He hoped he wasn't picked up by some psychotic couple. "How did you know I was out there?"

"I heard a crash and went out to see what happened." She shrugged. "Doyle and I carried you in. He was a medic in the Vietnam War. He thinks that, after some rest, you'll be okay. And then we'll get you home."

A medic would have known not to move someone that might have a spinal injury. And, from the sound of it, they wouldn't be bringing him to the hospital. He swirled the spoon through the soup again. His stomach growled, but he was still hesitant to consume anything these strangers cooked for him.

"I'm Cornelia, by the way." She stepped toward the door. "We'll be checking up on you periodically while you heal." Before she crossed the threshold, she turned back again. "If you need anything, don't be afraid to holler."

Brennan scooped some of the soup and lifted the spoon to his mouth. He waited a while after he swallowed to see if he'd experience any kind of strange effects.

When nothing happened, he ate the remainder and chugged the water, hoping for some relief for his pounding head.

⊷◇⊶

THE DISCOMFORT OF BEING in nothing but his boxers in front of two strangers was enough. But the strange man that examined him made the tension in the room feel like a rope about to snap.

Doyle's dark, sunken eyes matched the hue of his dusty suit. His gray hair matched the tie that hung from his wrinkled neck. He was a tall, thin man with scars on his hands and face. He applied pressure to Brennan's swollen leg with his bony fingers.

"It's not all that bad," Brennan said through his gritting teeth. He looked at Doyle to see if he'd picked up on his sarcasm, but the man's cold expression didn't change.

"This won't do," Doyle said in a flat, emotionless tone. "This won't do at all." He flashed his eyes to Cornelia, who stood at the side of the bed, and then back to Brennan's leg. His lips formed a thin line.

Brennan shifted his eyes to Cornelia and then to Doyle and back. "Maybe I should get to a hospital and get some x-rays."

"Oh, no," replied Doyle. He shook his head a bit. "You will be just fine here, Brennan. The swelling is bad, yes. But there is no discoloration. It's just some spraining. Mobility should be back to normal in time. You should consider yourself lucky." He stopped his probing and stood up straight.

"You don't think it would hurt to get a second opinion?"

Doyle lowered his face and looked at him from beneath his brow line. "Are you doubting my ability to examine your injuries?"

He looked away toward the wall. "No, I—I guess not."

"Good." Doyle turned to leave, but then turned to look at Cornelia. "Make sure our guest remains comfortable and his needs are met."

"Yes, sir," Cornelia replied to the man who'd already made his way to the other side of the door.

Brennan looked at the woman. "What's up with him? He looks like he's been through some shit."

She sighed and shrugged. "War is hell, I guess." She took a seat on the mattress next to him. "I don't know much about it other than he was separated from his unit and had to survive in the jungle for a while." Her eyes shifted to look out the now-dark window. "I think he's still dealing with whatever he went through, which is why he's a little strange."

"Are you his daughter or something?"

She laughed. "No, no. I have no blood relation to him. He found me, much like how I found you. Hurt and alone. But I didn't have anyone to return to once I got better, and he took a certain shine to me. So, I've just lived here with him all this time, helping him out with whatever projects he has going on."

Brennan pushed himself up to sit against the wall. "What kind of projects does he work on? He seems like an interesting guy, so I can imagine he must create some wild stuff."

She laughed. "Such a curious creature, you are," she said. "With all your questions." She gently rubbed his leg and stood. "I'll be right back. We're going to need to clean you up a bit." She ran her hand through her hair while she walked out of the room.

She came back a couple of minutes later, carrying a bucket of sloshing water by the handle with both hands. She set it on the floor next to the bed and sat down beside him again. "Okay. I'm going to wash you off." She smirked. "Don't worry, I'll keep it professional." Her fingers reached beneath the elastic band of his boxers.

"Wait, wait." He grabbed her hands to stop her. "Can't I just do this myself?"

"Don't be such a prude!" she said playfully. "This isn't the first time I'll be seeing a dick, and I mean, I'm only going to *wash* you."

He let go of her hands. "O—okay." He looked away when she pulled his boxers down the length of his legs, careful not to bump his swollen knees.

Cornelia reached into the bucket and squeezed the excess water out of the sponge she retrieved. She rubbed it along his skin, starting at his ankle and moving upward toward the indent of his hip. He shivered as the cold air touched his wet skin, but he could feel his body beginning to relax with the soothing glide of the sponge across his body.

She washed his chest and then his stomach. Then she gently moved the sponge over his penis. She rubbed the top of his penis gently before lifting it with her fingers and thoroughly washing its sensitive underside while it was lying on his stomach.

He cleared his throat a bit and tried to stifle the rush of blood with different, unrelated thoughts.

"I see someone is enjoying this a bit," she teased.

He looked down to see she was gazing at his almost fully erect penis. "Oh, I'm sorry." He felt heat rise in his face. "I just don't get touched like this all that much...unless it's myself." He laughed awkwardly. "And definitely not usually by a, uh, beautiful and mysterious woman." He cringed internally and wondered why the fuck he'd say something like that.

She put her wrist against her mouth and laughed. "It's okay. I'm glad you think I'm beautiful. I don't ever get complimented like that."

"Well, I mean..." He allowed his voice to trail off when he felt her hand grip his hardening shaft.

"Then I'm sure you won't mind."

He didn't say anything. He just closed his eyes and felt her slow strokes.

She slid her hand up and down a little faster.

"Fuck," he whispered.

Then he felt the warmth of her mouth on his tip. One of her hands then gently rubbed his balls, and another pinched and circled one of his nipples.

He opened his eyes to watch her head bob up and down on him. And it wasn't long before his load emptied into her mouth.

⫷◇⫸

CORNELIA CLIMBED FROM HER position on top of him, and Brennan scooted down the mattress so she could lay her head on his chest. The moonlight that came in through the window colored them in its blueish tint. He admired the curves of her naked body: the dip of her waist that rose into her hip, her small breasts and brown nipples, still hard.

"When I'm better," he said. "You should let me bend you over this thing."

She traced her finger along his chest. "I don't think you'll be here that long."

"Maybe we can stretch it out a little longer. So I can stay and have fun."

She met his gaze for a second and then looked away. "I don't know." She swallowed hard and sighed. "I'll probably never see you again after you're done here."

"Don't say that. I mean, we can keep in contact." He lifted his head a bit to look at her. "You know?"

She looked away. She made no attempt to hide the sadness that came over her face. Then she sat up and started slipping her legs back into her pajama bottoms.

"Where you goin'?"

"I can't be in here too late." She slipped her camisole over her head. "Doyle will kill me."

"Meet here again tomorrow night?"

She replied with a sad smile and quickly slipped through the door.

He stared at the ceiling for a while. He tried to remind himself that this was just a bit of fun, and it was just helping him to forget his suffering. He couldn't have anything beyond what he was having with this girl, not with the control that Doyle had over her that she hinted at.

He tried to sleep.

THE SEARING PAIN HAD become a dull whisper of discomfort in his legs. He could finally walk, though not without a bit of a limp, from the bed to the door. He could probably even walk himself to the bathroom now if he wanted to, but Cornelia would probably still want to help him. He would let her.

The thought of leaving her behind made him a little sad. He tried to remember that it was just because of the sexual attention she'd been giving him. But he couldn't help that he'd grown to like her.

Maybe he could talk her into finding a way for them to visit each other after he'd left.

"Good, good," said Doyle. His tone was too flat to indicate whether he actually approved of the situation or not. The man stood with his hands behind his back and monitored Brennan's movement. "Mobility has nearly returned to normal, and your swelling has disappeared entirely. Just another day or so, and you should be completely back to normal."

"Good." Brennan sighed. "I'm glad for what you've done for me. I'm grateful, really. But I can't wait to go home."

For the first time, Brennan saw Doyle's face struggle to smile. His lips revealed a set of brown and yellow crooked teeth. Some of them were broken and jagged. "Go home. Yes, yes," said the man, shaking his head. "Perhaps we can send you off with a dinner to celebrate your improved health."

Cornelia walked into the room. She approached with her hands behind her back. A smile pushed into the pale skin on her cheeks. "Brennan," she said. "I'm so glad you're almost better." She planted a soft kiss on his cheek and put her hands on his shoulders. She slid her touch down his arms and slid her fingers into his palms.

He felt his eyebrows twitch when he noticed she'd slipped a small piece of paper into his hand. He looked at Doyle and then quickly looked away and back to Cornelia. "Yeah, I guess I'll be able to leave soon."

"You will! And that's so great. I'm sure your loved ones have been wondering where you are."

He chuckled. "I'm sure they have been. They've probably already killed Justin for leaving me on the road like that to basically go missing."

Doyle made a noise that sounded like a small laugh.

Brennan made a motion with the hand that held the small piece of paper.

Cornelia flashed him a wide-eyed look and shook her head almost unnoticeably.

Doyle's face returned to its stone-faced expression. "Come, Cornelia," he said. "I'd like to speak with you for a moment in my office."

Oh, fuck. Brennan wondered if he noticed that she'd slipped him a note. He worried. He didn't know what this weird fuck would do to her.

She kissed him on the cheek and held his hands in front of him. Maybe he was some kind of jealous psychopath or something.

He considered following them. But Doyle had combat experience. He had desperate-man-surviving-in-a-jungle experience. He would know where to hit him to immobilize them. And then who knows what he'd do to *him?*

"Yes, sir." She followed him and shut the door behind her.

He unclenched his fist and looked at the paper in his open palm. He unfolded it and read her scratchy, obviously hurried handwriting.

I'm sorry about your friend Justin.

I really am.

Wait up for me tomorrow night.

I will bring you your clothes. Be ready.

He stared at the note. He read it again.

What the fuck?

⸻◆⸻

DOYLE SAT IN SILENCE. His scowl traced the scarred surface of his wooden desk. He looked at the buck knife that stood upright, stabbed into the surface on the opposite end of his lamp. Then he looked back to Cornelia and gestured to the wooden chair opposite the leather one on which he sat.

Cornelia sat as she was instructed. Her heart pounded against her ribcage.

Doyle made a pyramid with his fingers and stared at her.

Her eyes trailed to her hands, which were neatly folded into her lap. "What's the problem, sir?"

He pinched the bridge of his nose and let out a loud, long sigh. "What is going on?"

"Well..." She hesitated. She tried to collect her thoughts, to think of something to say. Nothing came. Nothing clever or convincing. "Well, what do you mean?"

"Look at me when I'm speaking to you."

Her face snapped up.

He scowled at her. He grabbed the buck knife and wiggled it free from the wood of his desk. He pushed the tip into the wood in front of him and then placed a finger on the tip of the handle. He spun the blade, drilling the metal into the wood. Then he picked up the knife and stabbed it into the desk again. "You *know* what I mean, Cornelia." He raised his head enough that more shadow could partially conceal his face. "Don't you fucking play dumb with me. What's going on with the boy?"

"I just…I just think he's a nice guy." She caught herself starting to look away and quickly shifted her eyes back to Doyle's. "I just think that we could, well, keep him."

"Keep him?" He smirked. "Like what? Like a pet?"

Her eyes lit up. She hated to word it like that, but she knew that might be able to convince him. "Yes! Like a pet, sort of. Look, I could just keep doing what I'm doing, and in return, he could, you know, help us with things."

Doyle chuckled. He nodded and ran a finger along the edge of his desk.

She watched, hopeful that he was considering her idea.

"So, you keep sucking and riding his dick, and then he will feel obligated to help us capture and process prey?"

"Well, we'd have to build him up to that, yes. Eventually, he could help us with that. But maybe he could help us with some other things in the meantime." *Like overpowering you when he's fully healed.* She hoped her expression didn't betray the thought.

He leaned back and folded his arms across her chest. "It does sound nice, yes. To have another man around who can handle some heavy lifting." He stroked a finger and thumb along his clean-shaven jawline. "But no." He wiggled the knife free again and pointed it at Cornelia.

She swallowed and stared at the blade's tip.

"We need to eat, Cornelia," Doyle continued. "An opportunity for something so young and fresh only comes along once in a great while. He was stupid enough to be captured by us. So, it's only right."

Her eyes welled with tears. She didn't dare look away or raise a hand to wipe them away.

"Don't forget what we are, my dear." He examined the blade and pricked his fingertip on its sharpened point. "And don't think I didn't see you slip something into his hand." His eyes narrowed. "If you're planning something with him, you'll both be on my plate for weeks."

A fire ignited in her stomach. Fear burned her inside.

"And you know," he continued. "There are consequences for such a thought-crime in my house, and you will have to be punished, regardless. So, here's what's going to happen if you want to keep your life."

She kept the stare of her widened eyes on him. She waited and listened.

———◆O◆———

HIS ANXIETY GREW WITH the darkness of night that eventually found its dominance over the room. He waited for hours. He quietly paced the room, testing how easily he could now walk.

He sat back on the bed. He draped the comforter over his cold shoulders. He dropped his eyes to the grain of the wooden floor and traced its barely visible pattern. Thoughts swam in his head.

He wondered what Cornelia meant when she wrote that she was sorry for Justin. He wondered what had happened to him. If Doyle killed him. And he wondered what she meant by telling him to be ready. Be ready for *what?*

He wondered when she would come explain it to him.

The door opened gently and quietly.

Cornelia stepped into the room. She was barefoot and carried her shoes in her hand. Her other arm cradled his clothes. She stepped carefully, as if she knew all the spots to hit so the floor wouldn't creak with her footfalls. She placed his clothes on the mattress. "Quickly," she whispered. "And quietly. Get it all on and let's go."

Brennan grabbed his clothes. He quickly slipped into them. "Where are my socks?" He realized he didn't have them after he slipped into his pants.

"Fuck. I don't know. But let's go. We need to go."

"It's the dead of winter. I'll freeze."

She gave him a hard look and grabbed him by the shoulders. "What is more important to you? Your toes or your life?"

"What?" He swallowed. The realization dawned on him. Doyle was going to kill him.

"Let's. Go."

"Okay."

He followed her out of the room and to the stairs. "I'm not going to be able to make it down these that fast."

Cornelia put a finger to her lips.

He limped down the stairs behind her. Some of them creaked. He saw her cringe at every sound.

They finally made it to the front door. Cornelia unlocked a double-cylinder deadbolt and opened the door.

The snow and ice that covered the porch felt like needles poking his feet. He felt his body scream to shrink back from the cold that bit through his clothes.

An old red truck sat in a gravel driveway. The driveway was connected to a dirt road that snaked into the darkness of the woods. He began making his way that way.

"What are you doing?" Cornelia whispered.

He turned to see her pointing to the surrounding woods.

He followed her into the trees. They broke into as best a run that he could muster. Frozen sticks and stray rocks stabbed at his feet. Logs hidden by shadows tripped him. The thin, cold air stung his lungs with his shallow, panted breaths.

A door slammed in the distance behind them.

"Come on," Cornelia said. "Keep up."

He could hear twigs snapping somewhere nearby. Heavy footsteps crunched the snow, following them at a walking pace. Doyle whistled a tune through his pursuit.

He used what energy he could muster to pick up his pace. He fought through the pain.

The woods ended at the pavement. The road had long been cleared of snow. He saw Cornelia heading for a building across the street. A long garage with a huge aluminum door at one end. He ran to catch up with her.

"Try the doors. Try the doors." She whispered fast between shortened breaths. "We can hide in here until morning. We'll be safe on the road in the day. Maybe get picked up by someone."

He tried a doorknob. Locked.

"Wait, wait."

He snapped his eyes to Cornelia.

"There's one over here."

She had a door opened down the side of the building. She slipped inside.

He jogged to follow her in. He quietly shut the door behind them.

The room was pitch black. The scent of copper hung heavy in the air. He fought to catch his breath and reached to find Cornelia. He pulled her close to him and held her. "Holy fuck," he said.

She shushed him. "We're not out of the woods yet."

He wanted to laugh at the irony of her euphemism, but he kept quiet.

Keys jingled. A lock disengaged. A light flipped on.

Brennan shut his eyes against the sudden burst from the florescent tubes in the high ceiling. When he opened his eyes, he saw Doyle standing in the empty garage. The man wore his old olive-drab military uniform. Streaks and pools of dried blood surrounded his feet. He picked up a large wrench from a nearby, blood-stained workbench.

Cornelia's face twisted into a defeated expression. She looked at Brennan before walking to stand next to Doyle.

"Bravo," said Doyle. "You can run now. And you are ready." He laughed. An insidious smile crawled across his face. "While it was a mock hunt, it was a fun hunt indeed.

"I'm sorry, Brennan," said Cornelia quietly. Her gaze drifted to the cement floor.

"Wait, so..." His voice trailed off. He began to sob. "Please," he begged. "I just want to see my family again. My friends. Please."

Doyle approached him. "Does the rabbit not want to return to its nest, only to have its plans foiled by the coyote?" He lifted Brennan's chin with a finger and then walked behind him.

"Please," Brennan whispered. He looked at Cornelia, who sniffled and wiped a tear away from her cheek.

He felt a heavy thud against the back of his head. The ground approached with his fall.

———◆◇◆———

HE OPENED HIS EYES and found himself seated at a dining room table. His head was pounding, and he felt like he might fade into unconsciousness again. He blinked and held his head up. His legs were throbbing. The pain was incredible. So much worse than after he'd been hit by the car.

A fire burned in a fireplace at the end of the room. Orange light bathed everything he could see.

Cornelia sat across from him. Blood trickled from an empty eye socket in her face. Her other eye stared blankly, traumatized.

Doyle sat at the head of the table. He made satisfied sounds as he ate from the same soup that was placed in front of Brennan and Cornelia. The soup looked and smelled the same as the soup he was fed the first day he woke up here.

He looked down at his legs. He found them both severed just below his knees. His stomach sank. He began to cry. "Please," he said quietly.

"Go on, then," Doyle said.

He looked back to Cornelia and then to the spoon that rested on a napkin next to his bowl.

"Eat," Doyle continued. He gestured with his own spoon. "I am excited for you to try my favorite dish. It's never tasted so sweet as it has with flesh as fresh as yours and your friend's." The man smiled with his broken teeth. Then he shoveled another spoonful of soup into his mouth.

Brennan picked up the spoon with a shaking hand. He looked at Doyle, who nodded. He scooped meat and broth and put the spoon into his mouth.

The contents swam across his tongue, and he fought a gag.
He swallowed.

6

THE INCIDENT AT SHORE RUN ROAD

THE RUST-LADEN HINGES CRIED as August opened her mother's closet door. She cringed. Her head snapped left. The hallway was still empty. If her father were to catch her, well, she didn't want to imagine the punishment.

Falling to her haunches, her knees thudded against the hardwood. Her breathing quickened. She inhaled the pungent odor of the forgotten fabric piled before her. A little mound like a vomit of colors faded by time and a layer of dust. With quick hands, she dug.

She knew it was here—it had to be. But where? She had heard these hinges cry when he'd slipped into this room. He *had* that book in his hand—the same journal her mother clung to.

She dug faster. She was running out of time.

There. She found a shoebox beneath the pile. It had to be here. She lifted the lid with trembling fingers. No. Empty. She pushed it aside.

"Come on," she muttered and dug into her pocket for her cell phone. "Come on." She tapped the screen with her finger. The flashlight whisked away the shadows. Smoothing her palm against the floor, she grazed the baseboard in the back corner with her fingertips.

A section of wood shifted with a clunk and fell forward. She hovered her hand with hesitation before reaching inside with a grimace. Cobwebs stuck to her flesh, and then she touched leather.

She studied the journal. Cracks crawled across the covers, and a leather cord kept the pages closed. She replaced the baseboard piece and tossed the clothes back atop the shoebox to their original, tangled form.

Standing, she shut the door and ran into the hallway. Her bedroom was just a few steps away.

SITTING CROSS-LEGGED ATOP THE white comforter, August opened the journal. The window next to her bed allowed sunlight between the slits of her blinds. The dimming ochre beam slithered across her carpet and up the wall across the room.

Finally, she would know the secret her parents had been hiding. She traced the handwritten lines with a finger and read aloud: "If we are to continue our operation, we must convince the ownership of the Sunset Motel on Shore Run Road to permit no further access to Room 206 save for our own."

With widened eyes, she swallowed hard. "What the hell?" she whispered. She looked out the window as a car rolled along the street below. The vehicle wasn't her father's. Good. She continued reading. "And we must maintain the success we have been having in keeping this quiet. What's been surprising is that this news hasn't leaked beyond our circle into the greater world outside of Coastalview, Maryland, save for the legend it has become."

She skimmed some writing and looked to the driveway below, still void of her father's Jeep.

"It's draw on the human psyche seems intensely powerful," she read. "So, the fact that a few among us have gathered in zealous worship comes as no surprise. We are to allow them this behavior. They will be most willing to keep it satiated—"

August set the journal down. She grunted in frustration at the fading light as the sun set. Running her hand through her black hair—her *mother's* hair, she thought with a smile—she made her way toward the light switch. She flipped it. A brief flicker gave way to fluorescent light that glowed yellow on the walls.

As she crossed the floor to return to her reading, she heard a muffled thud of a car door. "Shit," she muttered, peering out the window. Her father approached the front door. She ran back to her bed.

The front door squealed in the living room below. Keys clanged on the side table.

"August," that deep voice called.

She tossed the book inside her nightstand drawer, slid her legs beneath the comforter, ruffled her hair, and rested her head on the pillow.

Footsteps resounded on the hollow wood of the stairs, and a rap on her door soon followed. She kept quiet.

The knob shook, and the door opened. Her father walked into her room. "Hey, kid," he whispered. "Sleeping with the lights on?"

August rolled over and rubbed at her eye. "Hey, Dad," she replied with a faked rasp in her voice. She shrugged.

He wore his black slacks and a white button-down tucked into the waistband. A tie hung loosely from the collar, and a five o'clock shadow darkened his cheeks. "How was school?"

"It was school. You know."

Her father chuckled. "Of course, of course. I don't feel like cooking tonight." He raised his thick eyebrows. "You feel like having Chinese takeout?"

Shifting a bit, she widened her eyes. "Hell yeah! I'll never turn down Chinese."

A concerned look on his face faltered as a laugh broke through. "Watch it with the language."

"What? That wasn't even a big one."

"Yeah, yeah. I know. I remember being in eighth grade and thinking it was cool to swear." He allowed another chuckle. "Just never swore *to* my parents."

August grunted, rolling over.

She felt his approach, and he leaned down to place a kiss on the side of her head.

"Alright," he said. "I'll wake you when the food gets here."

"You're not going to pick it up?" said August, rolling back over.

His brows furrowed, and his hand smoothed his tie. "Why would I go pick it up when they deliver? Besides, I just got home from work. I don't really feel like driving again."

August attempted the puppy-dog eyes of innocent begging as best she could. "Not even to pick up Brandon? We wanted to go walk around town later."

He stood silent for a moment before expelling a sigh. "Not this Brandon kid again." He shifted his eyes toward the floor and formed a thin line with his lips. "Maybe. You know I don't like you hanging around boys, especially on a Friday night in the dark. Besides, I'm not sure Charlotte would be okay with you two running around town, either."

August twisted to retrieve a photograph of her mother from one of the cubbies built into her headboard. "Mom wouldn't have said no," she said. "*Alvah, the girl's getting older. Let her live her life. She'll be fine.*" Her impression was terrible, and she knew it.

He inhaled deeply, and his face became tinted with red. "August," he said and audibly exhaled. "Don't manipulate me like that. It's disrespectful to your mother's memory."

Nodding slowly, she allowed a moment of wordlessness and delicately traced the frame with her thumb, studying the photograph. It was taken during a family camping trip that she'd never forget. Her mother stood with a smile stretched to high cheekbones set in tanned skin. Her face was framed by thick black hair that fell toward a body shaped with hourglass curves—an image her own body began to mimic more and more. A large creek waterfall rained from a cliff behind her. She had that common, powerful stance. She *did* miss her, more than she could put into words.

Alvah sighed. "Look, it's okay. Just try to keep that in mind." His face betrayed a tempest of emotion, glossy eyes almost displaying a burden of guilt.

August remained silent, giving another nod.

"I'll just come get you when the food is here." He walked slowly from the bedroom, leaving the door open with his exit.

⬥

RICHARD CHEWED HIS LAST bite, looking at his watch. The hands indicated that the Sunday morning sun would be rising in a few hours. He pushed the empty plate an inch or so forward along the bar and placed his fork down on the edge with a clang that echoed through the empty Driftwood Diner.

He grunted and looked over the familiar surroundings. The walls were covered in chintzy ocean-themed décor, hung in no particular order, and there were faux starfish thrown onto the tables. Cracks splintered across the floor tile, and the windows had smears obscuring the night-bathed parking lot outside. The streaks magnified the red glow of the nearby motel sign. No amount of seafoam green cushions on the booth seats spewing stuffing from splits in the fabric could make this place feel comfortable.

His eyes shifted downward when he noticed the double door behind the bar swing open. The emerging woman ignored his cue to be left alone and approached. The fiery orange curls of her hair bounced with each step. She carried a carafe with care.

"More coffee, Richard?" she said, stretching her crimson lips into a smile.

"Thanks, Charlotte," he replied, waving dismissively. "But no."

"You know, for the little night owl you seem to be, you don't really drink much of this stuff." She twirled her curls with a finger.

"Don't need it. I'm up all night, anyway."

Charlotte made a throaty sound. "Me too. These damn night shifts are a killer."

Richard met her eyes for a moment. "Can't work the day shift?"

"No," she sighed. "Day shift is all full up." She narrowed her eyes, looking at something past him before her gaze returned. "I'm not really sure why we even keep this place running overnight anymore. It's not like anybody comes in this late besides you."

"Not even from the motel?"

She pursed her lips and shook her head. "Not many even stay there anymore. No vacationers. Nothin'. I don't understand it. It's a five-minute walk from the beach, and you can see the ocean from the back windows."

"Can't imagine *why*." He shrugged and took another glance around the diner.

She arched an eyebrow. "That sounds like you *can*. You're always hanging around here. What's up with it?"

Richard raised his fist with a protruding thumb, pointing over his shoulder. "Two-oh-six," he said and turned to look. Across the lot was the Sunset Motel. There were rows of dark windows and numbered doors in the wall along the empty lot. Behind a railing on the second floor were more.

A smile creased her lips, then morphed into a wide grin. Finally, laughter broke through. "Two-oh-six? Don't tell me you believe in that shit. I'd expect it from my teen son that lurks the internet in search of creepy urban legends, but you're a grown man."

Richard eyed the woman with raised brows. "Ever been in there?"

She wiped away a tear of laughter and composed herself. "No. For *safety* reasons. The floor's unstable—the broke asses just never fixed it. *That's* why."

A silent moment dragged between them, and Richard narrowed his eyes at her. Her body, in a split second, seemed to shift unnaturally—like the way things move beneath strobe light flashes. He shook his head. The lack of sleep must have been messing with his head. "I don't know if I believe that."

Charlotte raised a hand to her chest. "What, that I've never been in it? Or that they closed it because the floor's unstable?"

"That—" He turned to look at the sudden screech of skidding tires.

The square body of a dark SUV could be seen through the window. The driver's side door flung open, and the hazard lights flashed. A silhouette, tall and broad shouldered, emerged from the vehicle. The driver's door slammed with a muffle thud. He could see a gun in his hand and listened to him call into the dark. A single word that he couldn't make out. Maybe a name.

The man headed toward the motel.

Charlotte whispered something inaudible.

Unconcerned by her thoughts, Richard stood. He approached the door.

"*Richard!*" called Charlotte.

He stopped, turning to look.

"You're not going out there to confront him, are you?"

"Depends on what he's going out there to do," he replied, shrugging. "Doesn't look like anything good." He walked out of the diner.

⚬

The buzzing alarm screamed. August turned over to slam the button on top, and, with eyes half-open, allowed herself a few moments to lie in the dull red glow of the clockface numbers. Her morning routine was to give herself time to mentally prepare for the day.

Feeling her mind slip back toward slumber, she forced herself to sit. She placed her feet on the floor and crossed it to flip on the light. She yawned and opened her closet, tearing clothes from their hangers before starting for the bathroom.

She crept past the circular, decorative mirror on the wall in the hallway, but halted quickly, jumping as her father's bedroom door flung open.

"Why you up so early?" he asked with a confused expression. He was wearing his usual work clothes.

"Um, to get ready for school." She wanted to kick herself for the irritation in her tone.

"Kiddo, it's Saturday."

She stomped her foot. "Are you serious?"

Alvah chuckled. "Yep. Back to bed you go." He made a walking motion with two fingers and smiled. "I'll see you after my half-day shift."

Sighing, August turned to return to her bedroom.

As she got herself beneath the covers, daylight slipped in through her blinds. She tried to fall back to sleep, but she couldn't. She waited.

Eventually, sounds of footsteps jogging down the stairs were soon followed by the front door slamming closed. The engine noise was then lost to the distance. August sat up.

Retrieving the journal from the drawer, she flipped the pages to find where she'd left off.

She scrunched her face with concentration and traced her finger along the words. She began to read aloud: "We're uncertain of its origins, if any."

She fought a yawn that won, forcing its way up her throat. She then blinked away sleepy tears.

"And we certainly aren't interested in seeking the assistance of the scientific field. This would undoubtedly lead to government intervention. We only wish to keep it put, keep it appeased, as we are now required." She cocked her head. "Required? Required *how*?"

She looked out the window and shook her head. He was at work, but what if he forgot something? Paranoia, she thought. She just wanted to keep reading. Skimming a block of text, she continued.

"On the subject of its draw, we've hypothesized that once an individual has become aware of it, it has become aware of them.

From then on, they seem powerless against the need to seek it out. This proves the legends ultimately beneficial."

Another yawn emerged. She rubbed her eyes and propped her head with a pillow. Raising her legs, she rested the book against them.

"If we wish to prevent a similar event as such that befell the Wilmington family, we must keep it fed."

A newspaper clipping sat tucked between the pages. The headline was bold and sat above a block of text describing the disappearance of the Wilmington family, a mother and son, from the Sunset Motel. They'd been vacationing in Coastalview.

She continued reading the journal. "There has been some speculation that it seeks the destruction of human reproduction, considering its taste for women—they are the bearers of life. But we can't be certain about such specifics. We can only continue what we know to be effective."

"The feeding process is as follows:

"It seems as though its hunger is quelled by—"

The dense blackness of sleep swept August away.

———◆———

HER DAD'S VOICE DRIPPED with anger, waking her. "What the hell is this?"

"What, what?" replied August. She jumped upward, pushing the hair from her face. Her head shifted around quickly.

"Where did you get this?" He stood next to her bed, holding the journal with one hand. The leather string whipped around from the spine.

"I—I—" August began.

"I told you to stay out of that closet." Alvah's jaw bones protruded. His eyes burned with anger. "This is *my* journal. *My* writings."

"What?" she replied. "That doesn't even sound like you. *You* wrote that? I thought it was *mom's!*"

The fury grew on his face as the words spilled from her mouth. "Don't fuckin' worry about what it is."

August couldn't reign in her sudden anger. "Funny that it's about the same shit Brandon and I read about online, too."

Alvah raised his hand. A vein pulsed on his forehead.

She ducked from habit. Anger transformed into fear. Her arms raised to shield her face. "I'm sorry," she said. Tears pooled in her eyes. "I thought it was a story or something. It's creepy as hell. Please, Dad."

"Just—" He rubbed his forehead with the back of his hand. "Just stay the fuck out of that closet."

August watched him incline his head toward the ceiling. She could see worry replace the anger on his face.

He looked down at her. "You're grounded. And you're going to your grandmother's tonight. I'm meeting with a friend tomorrow, and you obviously can't be trusted to be here alone."

"What?" She slammed her hand against the mattress and almost lunged forward. "I don't want to go to grandmas! God, I hate it there. All because I found this stupid journal?"

"It's not—" Alvah reached into his breast pocket. He produced a pack of cigarettes. "You're going. That's it. No negotiations." His speech was muffled by the cigarette that dangled from his lips.

"But, what about Brandon?"

He huffed and removed the unlit smoke from his mouth. He pointed with the fingers that held it. "You're done hanging out with Brandon. Or any friends."

"But—" August's mouth snapped shut when her father raised his hand.

He stormed from the room with a slam of the door.

She hugged her legs and did nothing to stifle the tears rolling down her cheeks. She shouldn't have stolen the journal—she knew that. Curiosity just compelled her, *forced* her, and it only confirmed her suspicions. Her obsession solidified. The writing made the pieces fall together. She *had* to keep going. She craved more.

She slammed her fist against the pillow and drove her face into the fabric to grind a scream from her throat.

RICHARD PANTED AND INHALED the crisp air of the night as he ran. He rounded the corner of the motel. Just a little farther, and he might reach the man in time.

Up the metal stairs, he found him approaching the door. "Hey!" he called, running harder.

His feet halted. He crossed his arms over his face in useless defense. "Woah, woah." The silver barrel of a revolver aimed straight at him.

"Who the hell are you?" The man's knuckles whitened with a tightening grip on the pistol.

"I'm Richard," he replied. "Richard Wilmington. Just put the gun down."

The man stepped forward. His hand shook, but he maintained his aim. "For what? What the hell do you want?" Shadows crossed the man's scowl.

Death was inches from Richard's nose. He shakily gestured. "I just want to help. You don't know what you're getting into in there."

"I know what's in there."

"Then why are you going in?" Richard asked. "That gun won't do you any good."

The man's forefinger shifted to the trigger. "My fucking daughter is in there. And now *you're* in my way."

"Okay, okay," Richard's hands shot upward, palms out. "Listen, man. This thing's taken family from me, too. Let me come in there with you."

"So, you can just knock me out and feed me to it?"

"It doesn't work like that. So, no. I've figured out how to deal with this thing. Trust me."

The man finally lowered the gun. "Alright, Wilmington." He gestured toward the door with the barrel of his gun. "You first, then."

Slowly, Richard stepped forward to the door.

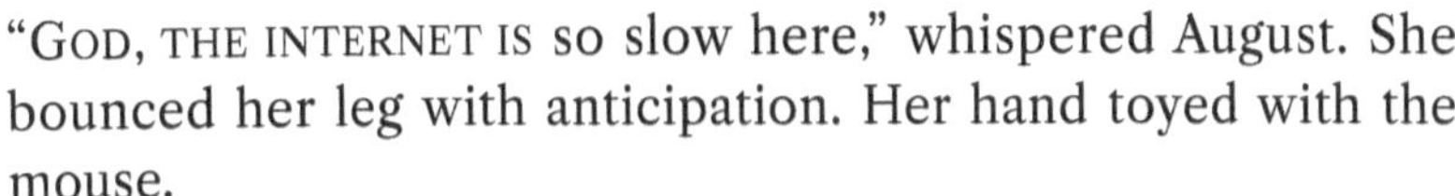

"GOD, THE INTERNET IS so slow here," whispered August. She bounced her leg with anticipation. Her hand toyed with the mouse.

The desktop screen remained white; a loading wheel displayed on the tab.

"Come on. Come *on*." She turned her head toward the open door. Her grandmother's snoring stopped. She listened carefully, but there were no approaching footsteps from the hall.

Finally, the page began loading. Text etched downward on the screen and wrapped a grainy image. It was all beneath a bold, black title, similar to the one in the newspaper clipping:

THE INCIDENT AT SHORE RUN ROAD: WHAT LIES IN THE DEVOURING REFLECTION

Squinting, she skimmed the author's speculations about an unnatural culprit and a surviving son that has faded into obscurity.

As she scrolled, a blurry image of a woman standing in a room struggled to load. She looked a lot like Brandon's mother. *She couldn't be*. Charlotte would have been much older by now.

Her eyes flashed to the clock on the screen. "Shit," she said and jumped to her feet. Brandon would be left stranded in the dark if she didn't leave now.

She peaked her head through the door and checked the hall. The flash of a television could still be seen from her grandmother's room. Her snoring could be heard again. She tip-toed toward the front door.

<hr>

AUGUST WALKED THE SHOULDER of Shore Run Road until the trees gave way to the slab of pavement painted with uninhabited parking lines. Keeping close to the motel, she made her way past the dark and empty reception office. She could almost feel the electric tingle of the vacancy sign, enveloped in its red glow. Her heart raced with nervous excitement.

She raised the cell phone to her ear. There were a few rings until Brandon answered. "Hey," she said. "Got past Gram without her even noticing. I'm here. Where are you?"

"*I'll be there soon,*" Brandon buzzed from the other end. "*You know where to go?*" His breath was labored. August could tell he was walking quickly.

"I know the opening is—what—a window in the back?"

"*Yeah, it's like a basement window,*" he replied. "*Just go in. I'll meet you when I get there.*"

"Okay. See you soon." She tapped the screen to end the call.

She lifted her hood and looked toward the diner. Brandon's mom was distracted, chatting with some guy. She would be okay if she hurried and moved further into the shadow of the structure.

Once behind the motel, she checked her surroundings. Dumpsters sat across from the back wall, decorated with graffiti tags. She followed the corner to the basement window. She approached.

She knelt and reached for the window sash, sliding the lower pane to the top. She found the ease with which the window opened surprising. *Why wasn't there more effort to keep people out if the rumors were true?*

She hesitated. Maybe she should just wait for Brandon. What if a squatter lived in that room? Maybe the two of them would stand a chance together. She doubted that either of them could take on someone like that alone.

No. She needed in here. The blackness before her called—reached toward her with an invisible, beckoning finger. She slipped through the window into the shadows.

Her feet slapped against concrete, shattering the silence and echoing through the open space. The flashlight on her phone struggled to illuminate anything other than a thin line of floating dust. A small circle of colorless light fell onto the stained concrete wall some distance away.

She walked forward, slowly. Her heart pumped in her ears. Ahead, she could see a break in the wall. A narrow passage. She could fit if she turned sideways.

A sudden, loud slam came from behind. She spun around to see Brandon behind the closed window, his reddish-blonde strands of hair fallen over his face.

August charged over. "Brandon!" she called. "What are you doing?"

"Go through the wall," he replied with a voice muted a bit by the glass.

"No, come in."

"Go through!" Brandon laughed. "Find the ladder." He motioned with two fingers, like legs climbing upward.

"Please!" August cried. She didn't care about the tears wetting her face now.

Brandon rolled his eyes. "Oh, my god. You're such a pussy. Just go. I'll come in after you go up."

"I'm *not* a pussy!"

"*You're* the one crying. Go!"

She turned, shining her flashlight to the crevice. She inched forward with trembling legs. Placing her arms tight against her sides, she turned her body, slipped her phone into her pocket, and entered.

The space was tight, with only a few inches between her face and the wall. Without the guidance of her flashlight, she side-stepped, blind in the darkness. After each shaken exhale, her breathing grew closer to panic.

She slid her palms along the cold wall. Finally, they touched the rungs protruding from the concrete. She began a shaky climb.

The concrete transformed into a plaster wall. Cracks slithered across the material to reveal planks of rotting wood. Stringy hairs hung from the edges of the plaster.

An opening awaited at the ladder's end. Like a gaping mouth, the hole housed a material black and breathed cold air. She stared into it for a long moment before crawling inside with a shiver.

Her knees scraped against a wooden floor as she crawled. The short tunnel ended at a small door. She pushed the door open and retrieved her cellphone. The thin glow of the screen illuminated the black and white tile floor of the kitchenette. She had emerged from a cabinet covered in peeling white paint. A musty odor hung in the air. She could taste the dusty atmosphere.

Carpet sprawled beyond the linoleum. The bedroom housed two double beds with colors dimmed by a thick, webby film. A dresser sat across the room, topped with an old television, black screened and cubical. August stepped further inside.

She noticed motion from a corner and jolted quickly in its direction. Her reflection mirrored back in a tall, wide, and frameless mirror leaning against the wall. A crack splintered from an upper corner, crawling across the glass like black lightning.

She stepped toward her own image. The light on the surrounding papered walls swelled with each forward inch. They seemed to house a subtle blue tinge. The colors undulated, breathing. August shook her head—this must have been a trick of the eyes in the dark.

She turned. Or, she thought, she turned. The mirror still stood there. She turned again. The mirror was still there. The glass traveled to envelop her until she felt boxed in with her reflection on all sides. The same image of herself standing in that dark room, surrounded by the dull blue light.

She dropped onto her haunches and tried to calm her breathing. She clenched hair and cried. Tears fell like rain to her lap.

Then she heard her name. A distant whisper rasped like it had come from struggling vocal chords.

She lifted her wet eyes. A shape moved from beyond the blue light, an image appeared. She recognized her mother and shot to her feet.

She wiped her cheeks with her wrist. "Momma?"

Momma stopped and stared with drooping eyes. Thick black hair fell in wiry strands to her bare shoulders, framing a blank, emotionless face.

She studied her mom. She wore a tattered brown camisole and jeans. Bruises spotted her arms. Blood traced a line from the corner of her mouth.

"Mom?" she reiterated. "What's wrong? What happened to you?"

Elongated appendages, shriveled bony fingers coal black in hue, appeared at the side of momma's head. They laid slowly, one-by-one, across her face. One deadened eye peered between them. Her mouth was left exposed. Another hand wrapped around her torso, appearing in the same fashion.

"Mom!" screamed August. She ran to the mirror and pounded her fists against it.

The woman's eye widened. Her lips quivered. She struggled to speak.

Swallowing against sobs, she tried to focus on what this caricature of her mother might say.

"*Heeeee*," she droned, straining. "*Heeeeee*." The fingers that wrapped her face and stomach shifted and twitched.

August turned, and she saw her father. He looked blurred—fuzzy—a distorted video image. He stood with the man Brandon's mom talked to in the diner.

"Dad?"

He didn't answer and turned to speak to the man. No sound came from his mouth. "Dad!" she screamed. "Dad, no!"

ALVAH RAN HIS FINGERS along the motel's siding. There it was. He bent the vinyl outward, and a key fell into his palm.

Richard's face twisted with inquisitiveness. Then he shook his head. "When we get in there," he said. "Don't look in the mirror."

Alvah didn't look at him. "Wasn't planning on it." The deadbolt gave a click and he opened the door.

As they moved through the entry, a rhythmic thudding grew in volume. Alvah knew the source, and he was sure that Richard did, too.

"I didn't know that door still functioned," said Richard. "Thought they sealed it off."

"Those that know, know. Those that don't, they go below." He replied, sighing. "I wish I didn't."

Richard turned back for a second, studying Alvah. "And why do you know?"

He gave no reply. He just pointed toward the room with the barrel of his gun.

Richard turned and continued walking.

Alvah winced at the sight of August banging her body against the mirror repeatedly, arms limply swaying at her sides. She babbled incoherently. He pressed a fist against his forehead.

"It's sick," whispered Richard. "This thing."

Alvah didn't reply. He just continued staring as August turned.

With a tilted head, she looked with blank eyes at him; her stare agonizing, or maybe pleading. A trembling moan poured from her slacked and drooling mouth.

"We have to kill it." Richard's voice was shaking. "Get rid of it."

Alvah turned his head. "Yeah? And how do you suppose we do that?"

"A garbage bag to wrap the mirror. And fire."

He shook his head and laughed, feeling a flash of adrenaline. Blood surged through his veins. "Are you serious? You can't."

Richard took one backward step. Fear flooded his eyes.

Alvah put the barrel of his weapon in Richard's face. He bit his lip and pulled the trigger. The sound of August's groaning accompanied the gunshot. Dead weight hit the floor with a thud.

He turned and stared at his daughter down the sights of his pistol. With a quick glance at the mirror, he recognized the figure within. She had the same dead eyes as August.

"Katrina," he whispered. Tears trickled to wet his cheeks. His hand shook.

He squeezed the trigger, and August fell. Her blood and chunks of gray matter painted the walls as the bullet found its exit from the back of her head.

He approached the door, wracked with tremors, and listened to the crunching glass and the wet slurp of the slithering something in the room behind him as he exited.

⬥◦⬥

ALVAH LOWERED HIS HEAD to the counter in the Driftwood Diner, half-consciously tapping his finger against the surface. The white linoleum looked gray in the early morning hours.

The double doors of the kitchen swung open. Charlotte emerged, carrying a carafe in one hand and a mug in the other. She approached with gleeful, bouncing steps. "Hey, honey," she said, setting the mug onto the counter. The room filled with aroma as she filled it. "Good thing you left your keys in your Jeep. I pulled it into a spot for you."

Alvah gave no reply. He only continued gazing at the mug, wordless and numb.

"You're welcome." Charlotte had an edge to her tone. She set the carafe down with a bit of force.

After a long pause, he said, "Charlotte." His voice was gravelly. Without an upward glance, he grasped the handle of the mug and dragged it toward himself.

"Oh, perk up." Her brows furrowed with irritation. "Think of all the good things that come from this: it stays fed, we help it grow, and it loves us for it." Laughter trickled from her. "And, boy, is Brandon growing into his own as a little disciple. What a perfectly executed plan." She bent at the waist and leaned her elbows on the bar. "And, I'll have you know, that boy came up with it all on his own, knowing how drawn little August was."

Alvah lifted his face and glared. "My fucking daughter is dead."

"More or less." She gave a pronounced shrug and tilted her head. "And if we hadn't done this now, how long would you have taken to step up?" A wicked smile pushed at her porcelain cheeks. "We both know how you dragged your feet with Katrina." She gave a pause and exhaled. "And I don't have to ask about the last Wilmington. I didn't see him come back out. Good." She smiled.

Nodding slowly, Alvah sipped from the mug and winced at the heat that slid down his esophagus. "I think I'm out. I can't fucking do this anymore, and I've already done too much. Far too much."

"Oh, no, my sweet boy." She extended her finger and brushed Alvah's jawbone with a talon-like ebony-painted fingernail. "There is no out of this." She shifted with an unnatural motion, a glitched shudder.

"Then what next?" He bit at her with his words.

She stood straight and looked downward at him. "You've got more family left. But I'll give you a few years. Just like I did with Katrina and August. In the meantime, you let that journal float around. We need more. Let the legends spread."

Alvah averted his eyes. His mother would be the only one left to give.

"Now," continued Charlotte. "My shift is almost finished here, and the sun is almost up. People are going to be showing up for breakfast soon, so you need to go home. Get yourself cleaned up and get some rest." She patted his shoulder and walked away, disappearing behind the kitchen doors with a strut.

———◄O►———

ALVAH STOOD AT THE top of the hillside that overlooked the coast behind the Sunset Motel. He watched the waves of the Atlantic crash against the shore to drag sand into the depths. The sun hung in the sky and left a trail of light across its surface. He forced a sigh.

There would be no more of this, he thought. His mind traced a line to memories of chances from when he could have run. He could have taken his wife and daughter elsewhere, after the discovery of the reality of this place.

Useless. It would have been useless. Charlotte would have come for them.

He ground his teeth at the thought of the terror living in the building behind him—the terror that he would never be able to separate himself from.

Retrieving his cell phone from his pocket, he sifted through the contacts and found his mother's name. There was ringing on the other end.

"*Hello?*" the woman answered.

"Hey, Mom," replied Alvah.

"*Did you find her?*" she asked. "*Have you checked Shore Run Road? She was reading this article online. It was on the computer when I noticed she was gone.*"

Alvah was quiet for a moment. Now she knows. "Listen. Mom." He sighed into the phone. "It's especially important now that you listen. I need you to get out of here. Go stay with Uncle Sheldon in Maine and *never* come back here. Do you understand?"

"*What? Why?*"

"Promise me," he replied with trembling words. "Promise me now."

"*O—okay, honey. If it's that serious.*"

"I love you." Alvah removed the phone from his ear and tapped its screen. "You live," he whispered.

From the waistband of his jeans, he wiggled the gun free, lifting the barrel to his temple. This was *necessary*, especially now.

"I'm sorry, Katrina. I'm sorry, August. More than you'll ever know, I'm sorry." His gaze never wavered from their appreciation of the beauty below as he thumbed the hammer backward. "Mom, you live," he repeated.

He clenched his teeth and pulled the trigger.

7

TO TASTE HER FLESH

ANGELINA SAYS IT'S NORMAL to be angry when someone close to you dies. *Kicks the bucket*, as she likes to put it. But I wasn't sure about the path I was headed down.

My good friend's funeral came and went like any other. A service full of sobs and words from friends and a preacher. A burial directly after, where mourners placed beautiful flowers on top of the casket. Then, the wake, where half-assed store-bought sandwiches are served, and people laugh about all the funny stuff that person did while they were alive.

I left early and found myself back home. The comfort of sitting at my kitchen table, drinking a cup of coffee, and gathering my thoughts didn't have its usual effect. My living room felt emptier than ever, even though the number of occupants remained the same. I thought of going into the basement and reorganizing those stupid weights. Maybe the exercise I'd get from the weight bench I bought and never used would help get some of these feelings under control. But I couldn't muster the energy. And, finally, my bedroom waited for me like a coffin of my own, where I wanted to go for that long sleep that no one wakes up from. I didn't want to feel the pain I was feeling now.

I looked at the mannequin that stood in the corner. I'd usually dress her in beautiful clothing that I'd bought just for her. It was a fun activity. A little hobby that kept my mind occupied in lonely hours.

I tried staring at her, planning her shirts and pants or a nice little dress. I thought about what great accessories would go with what outfits. But even that brought me no comfort.

I just stared at her while my mind drifted elsewhere.

Maria was a good woman. And I missed her. I saw her just a couple of weeks ago, and I wished against all wishes that I could go back and relive it. I wished that I had told her about my true feelings, even if she thought I was a total creep and never talked to me again. At least, then, she would have known.

She stood in line at the coffee shop in front of me. I begged her not to pay for my drink and quiche. They were expensive, but she insisted.

"I don't know what to do about him, Chris," she said when we sat down. She toyed with the lid of her cup and then with one of the many pendants she owned that dangled from one of the many chains she adorned. I could see the sadness in her eyes as she looked down at her drink, barely touching it. "Mark's been so awful to me lately."

I listened to her intently, as I always did.

"I try to try to think of what I could have possibly done wrong, but—"

"You haven't done anything wrong," I interjected. I reached my hand across the table to rest it on top of hers. God, I could have sworn I felt electricity shoot into my palm every time I touched her. "Sometimes people just sour."

"I don't think he's soured." Her tone carried an edge of defense. She still loved Mark, of course. Even if I couldn't possibly figure out what it was that she saw in him. The man was slobby. He had no drive to better himself or their future together. The type of person that just punched a time clock, came home, slept, and repeated the process the next day. Not to mention the mouthful of crooked teeth I wanted to knock down his throat every time I saw him. This wasn't the first time I'd heard complaints about him of this nature from her. Mark *was* sour—he always was. He only got worse over time.

"I just feel like he's started to hate me over the past few months," she continued.

I quickly shifted my grimace to my best comforting expression. "How in the world could *anyone* hate you?"

"We've been fighting a lot." She sighed and tucked her dark hair behind her ear. I could tell she was fighting back tears. "He's just been horrible to me. Mean and distant."

"That doesn't sound like very healthy behavior." I sipped my coffee to wash down the bite of quiche I'd finished chewing while listening. "Maybe he is having problems at work. He could be taking them out on you. I've read that people tend to take those things out on the people closest to them. It's 'cause they don't think they're going anywhere." I shrugged. "But you could. If he keeps acting like that."

Her eyes became knives meant to cut me. My toe-dip in her pool found the water too cold. I realized I'd have to be more tactful with my suggestions. "I'm sorry," I continued. "If it were ever to come to that."

She sighed. "It's okay. I understand what you mean." Her eyes fell to her coffee cup. "I mean, you're not the first person that's said that. I just couldn't imagine leaving."

I just couldn't imagine leaving. Knives to my stomach. I swallowed against the pain and tried to keep any sour expression from forming on my face.

Maria had no idea how badly I pined for her. She was clueless about the amount of restraint it took to keep my engagements with her respectful. I often wanted to surprise her with my lips pressed to hers. What sparks could fly if she'd only let them ignite inside her.

I gently lifted her chin with two of my fingers. "Focus," I said with a chuckle. "Do you have any idea why he might be treating you like this suddenly?"

Her eyes darted downward again, and she stayed quiet for a few moments. "I know that having a family isn't for everyone. I... I don't know. I just hoped that I could sway him." She scratched a fingernail against the lid of her coffee cup. "It's just that it's too late now. And I guess I've been a little harsh on him about it."

"Maria, anyone would be lucky to have a family with you. And it'd be a beautiful family at that. But what do you mean it's too late now?"

Again, she gave me silence. This time, she drew it out longer. I knew when she was avoiding something.

"Maria, what's going on?"

Her lip trembled. She inhaled deeply. She looked away until the flush in her cheeks subsided. Then she looked back at me.

I exhaled sharply through my nostrils.

"He got a vasectomy without even talking to me first."

I felt a hand balling into a fist beneath the table. I physically bit my tongue. "That's...that's horrible. I..." I grunted. "Is there anything I can do?"

Quiet tears rolled down her cheeks. Her glassy, beautiful eyes looked at me as if to beg for my help. I wanted to tell her that I loved her. That I loved her for a long time. I wanted to tell her that I would gladly give her children if that's what she wanted. But I didn't. I kept my mouth shut. And I regretted it.

Would she still be alive if I'd told her?

No one confirmed her cause of death yet. But I knew. I knew what happened. I knew that suicide gripped her in those hopeless moments. (I'd be suicidal if I were married to that piece of shit, too). She gave in to the call. Beyond the shadow of a doubt, I knew.

I zoned back to my current surroundings. This quiet bedroom hugged me with its silence. My mannequin stared back at me with her plastic, eyeless face. And I wished she were Maria.

I stood from my bed and stretched my arms high above my head. I clasped my hands together, lacing my fingers, exhaled, and lowered them back to my sides. I wiggled my toes and felt the floor beneath the soles of my feet.

Maybe a shower would help me clear my head.

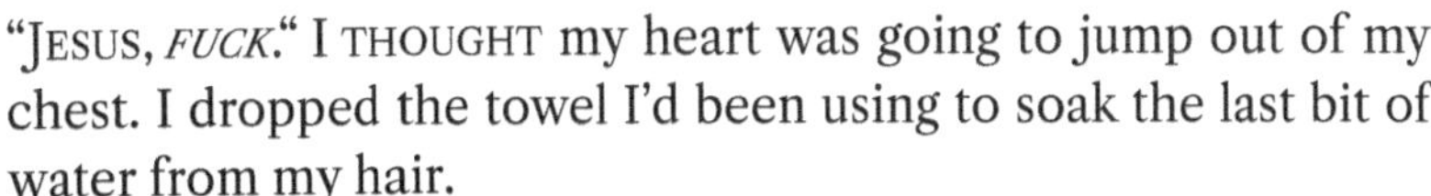

"Jesus, *FUCK*." I thought my heart was going to jump out of my chest. I dropped the towel I'd been using to soak the last bit of water from my hair.

Angelina lay smiling at me on my bed. Her strawberry blonde hair lay gracefully over her shoulders and exposed chest. Her pale, slender legs stretched across the comforter from beneath one of the red, lacy nighties I sometimes dressed my mannequin in.

"When the fuck did you get here?"

She giggled playfully. "I let myself in. I heard the water running when I was looking for you, so I figured I'd surprise you."

My hand still rested on my chest like it could slow the pounding of my heart. "Well, you scared the ever-living shit out of me."

She pushed her head back into the pillow and stretched an arm across the mattress. "*No*," she said, smirking. "What I *did* was get your blood pumping."

"You certainly succeeded there." I rolled my eyes.

She sat up and patted the bed. "Come over here with me." Her puppy eyes and pouty lips begged me to come closer.

I shook my head and dropped my gaze to the floor. "I'm not really in the mood, Angelina."

"I could *put* you in the mood."

"No. No, I don't think you can."

I was never in the mood when she did this. She often showed up unannounced. This scenario was usually the same. I'd leave to get groceries or take a walk or even leave the room for a while like I had just done, and she'd just be somewhere in the house waiting to scare me and then tempt me.

In fact, the entire thing always puts me in a worse mood than I may have already been in.

And I didn't want her the way she wanted me. She was always a good friend in great times of need. Her validating ear was one I'd never refuse to pour my troubles into. The few times I allowed her to *hand me a favor* in times of loneliness left me feeling guilty and strange. So, I wanted to put a stop to it. She kept showing up, though, wanting more and more from me.

She dragged out a groan. "I know you miss your Maria, Chris. I can take your mind off her."

That stung. "Take my mind off the woman I loved?" I scowled. "She killed herself, Angelina. I don't want to take my mind off her. I want to remember her fondly." I turned and toyed with my mannequin's jewelry that I left lying on my dresser.

"Well, if you're going to dwell, I can *be* her for you."

I scoffed. What an insult to my pain. "Yeah, I'd love to see your plan for how you'd do that," I muttered. "A wig and some makeup, and you'll jump out from behind the closet door to scare me like the ghost of my dead woman of interest." I slid a thin gold chain between my thumb and forefinger. The piece of jewelry was one I'd originally bought for Maria but, in my desperate fear of rejection, decided to give to my mannequin instead.

"Turn around."

I snapped my head upward and furrowed my brow. I then set the necklace down and turned to face Angelina again.

"Stop it." I felt the heat rise in my face. Tears welled in my eyes. My mouth twisted into the features of an onset of sobbing. "It's not right." I pinched the bridge of my nose and squeezed my eyes shut.

"Christopher," she said in that gentle tone. That tone that danced in my ears was like the way the reach of the tide danced between my toes. A tone that caressed my heart like that comforting rustle of leaves when the wind picked up at the arrival of a summer evening storm. The tone Maria used calmed my nerves in moments of anxiety. "It's okay. Come, be with me." Her voice *was* Maria's.

And she now looked like her, too. Those strawberry blonde strands transformed into silken raven black, thick and straight. Her figure morphed into gentle curves that my hand *pleaded* for *years* to explore. Her breasts, grown, threatened to tear through fabric now sizes too small for them. Her thin lips became plump and red and kissable. Even her eyes changed to that forest green, their lids shrouded in smoky makeup that suggested dark mysteries of passion I'd longed to seek.

I hesitated. But then my legs carried me forward as if by their own will.

"Let me hold you."

I knelt on the bed and crawled to the side of the woman I've loved for so long. I rested my head onto her arm, against her shoulder. I listened to her slow breathing and savored the sweet scent of her.

Her fingers trailed soft designs along my scalp. She shushed me as tears burst from my eyes, and I gripped her waist with an angry hand.

"It's okay to be angry about what happened," she whispered. "It's okay."

"No, it's not." My voice cracked through my crying. "What am I supposed to do?"

"Whatever you feel is right."

I clenched my jaw and breathed faster through my teeth.

"I know, I know." Her fingers dug with soft scratches on my head. She shushed me some more.

I kissed her neck. I pressed myself harder against her.

"Not yet."

I lifted my head and looked at the Maria facsimile. I watched as the woman transformed back into Angelina. I sat up, and I forced my face into my palms. I cried harder. "Why?"

"Look at me." Angelina lifted my chin so my bloodshot eyes could meet the clear blue of hers. "You can have Maria when you have quenched this deep anger." She grinned at me.

I wiped my face and nodded before I fell back into her arms. "I will do anything," I whispered. With my head nestled into her breast, I quietly cried until my exhaustion took me.

I OPENED MY CLOSET door. An assortment of brilliantly colored fabrics formed a collage of nearly endless choice in front of me. But my indecisive nature always made this task seemingly monumental. Nothing seemed good enough. Especially now. But still, I didn't mind as much today. I felt sort of reinvigorated.

I flowed to the sounds of Bach sung by my radio. I sifted through my collection, wondering what would bring out the best features of my mannequin without being too repetitive of recent outfits. Lace, cashmere, and silk. All too much to pick from. All too lovely.

Angelina brewed coffee in the kitchen—or at least she watched the pot of coffee that I, of course, had to start for her—and the aroma wafted its way upstairs. I inhaled the scent and sighed half-happily. Maybe the break and the caffeine would shift my focus so I could come back to the clothes re-freshed.

A fist pounded on my front door. I huffed at the interruption.

"Angelina," I called. "Can you get that?"

She didn't answer.

The knocking continued.

"Of course not," I muttered before making my way downstairs.

Angelina stood oblivious in the kitchen when I passed. She still wore the red gown she had on last night. I thought I heard her humming along to the muffled melody from the radio, but I brushed it off.

I peered through the peephole and saw Mark standing on my porch. His rust-colored hair looked disheveled, and stubble marred his pale cheeks. He held a large cardboard box in his arms.

I grimaced and hesitated. I really didn't want him in my house. But curiosity impelled me. So, I reached for the knob and waited a second before turning it and opening the door. "Can I help you?" I said.

Mark gave me a tired half-smile. "Hey, buddy. How are you holding up?"

Buddy. I scoffed internally. No, cringed. As if I could ever be this man's buddy. "I am doing as well as anyone could be in these circumstances."

"Trust me. I understand." He shifted the box in his arms. "Do you mind if I come in?"

How could he have possibly understood? He didn't love Maria the way I did. He didn't care for her, listen to her, consider her perspective on anything. He took her for granted. Treated her terribly. Made her sad enough that she felt her only escape was death. God, I wanted to reach my hand into his mouth and tear his tongue out where he stood just for saying something like that.

"This is heavy." He shifted the box again.

Don't you dare get short with me. "Sure. A new pot of coffee just finished. You can set that on the kitchen table." I gave him a thin-lipped smile and gestured permission to enter.

"Thank you." He walked past me and through the living room, and I followed him.

I moved a half-drunk bottle of red wine from the table onto the counter next to my set of knives to give him space to set the box down.

He pulled a chair and sat, and then he pushed the box toward the side of the table for what I'm assuming was so we could make eye contact.

I poured two cups of coffee. His into my least favorite mug. "Do you take any sugar or cream?"

"I'll bet he'd take lots of Benadryl in his," Angelina interjected, with a whisper into my ear.

I flashed her a *look*.

"Remember what I said last night," she continued, but in Maria's voice.

I shuddered and inhaled.

"Just a little cream, thank you," Mark said.

I finished fixing our drinks and set his in front of him before I sat down across the table.

He looked at the box. "I was pretty reluctant to part with these," he said. He scratched his head and puffed an exhale. "But I know you two were very close friends, and I figured this would make you feel better."

I sipped my coffee and waited to hear whatever grand gesture he was going to make to make me feel better about the love of my life killing herself over this asshole. What arrogance.

"I know that you have that hobby. She told me." He shifted his gaze to look past me for a second, and then brought it back to my unwavering stare. "Where you like to dress that mannequin you have. So, I figured you'd like to have these."

I looked at the box, and I tapped a fingernail against my mug. My stomach caught fire. If he was going to say what I thought...I might break down at this table.

Mark slowly opened the box and pushed it toward me. The container was filled to the top with carefully folded clothes. The top layer being the black camisole Maria wore the last time I saw her. I felt my lower lip move with an involuntary quiver, and I inhaled slowly and deeply to fight the tears that tried to force their way beyond my eyelids. "Oh, you—you shouldn't have." I gently caressed the fabric.

"It's okay. Really." He sipped his coffee. "Whatever is in here that I found in the hamper has been washed and dried."

I cleared my throat and looked at him with widened eyes. "Oh. How very, um...how considerate of you."

I brought my fingers to my chewing teeth while I watched him dig through the contents of the box.

"Shit." He rubbed his head. "I thought I put her necklace on top. Maybe it fell in here somewhere." He continued digging.

I gently pulled the box away from him. If I kept letting him dig through them, he'd get his disgusting scent and dandruff all over these important clothes he'd already damaged with his washing machine. "It's okay. Just bring it if you find it."

"Oh, look at that," Angelina muttered. "He made sure to get her scent off them *and* he's ridding himself of precious memories of her." She chuckled. "You know, now would be the perfect time to kill him, Chris. Doesn't that just throw you over the edge?"

I tried my best to ignore her, giving her a brief sidelong glance before returning my attention to Mark.

"Of course," he said. "That's not a problem."

Angelina chimed in again. "Or he's just taunting you. Have you considered that?"

"Stop it!" I turned to Angelina and cut the air with my hand.

"Is this a bad time, Chris?" asked Mark almost sheepishly. "I'm sorry." He darted his eyes back and forth between me and Angelina.

"It's okay. Don't mind...*her*."

He stood from the table. "You know, I should get going any-way." He pointed a thumb toward the living room. "I need to keep myself pretty busy these days. I just wanted to drop these off for you."

"Okay. I understand." I wanted to internally berate him for coming into my house, having me make him a cup of coffee, and then leaving after having barely touched the beverage. But I was too excited about the clothes to care. So, I escorted him through the living room and opened the front door. "Please. If you find that necklace, would you mind bringing it over to me?"

He looked past my head and then at me. "Sure thing."

"Thank you." I shut the door and returned to the kitchen.

Angelina scoffed. "You really blew that one."

"It was because of *you* that I lashed out like that and scared him away." I dumped the coffee Mark sipped down the drain and threw the mug directly into the trash. I wouldn't *ever* drink from it again.

"You might not get a chance like that again. After your little hint of domestic abuse toward me, he'll probably never come back."

I snatched the box from the table and turned to her with a fiery expression. "Do you want me to put these on you or not?"

She stared at me, wordlessly, with that smug, chiseled plastic expression.

"My goodness," I said, raising half-curled fingers to my lips. "You look so beautiful in this lighting."

Jarred candles on the nightstands waved with flames in mimicry of my passion. Their scents accentuated the sight in front of me.

"And those *clothes*." I bit my lower lip and sounded a primal grunt.

In full Maria form, Angelina sprawled across the bed, dressed in only the black camisole and a gray pair of boy shorts that hugged her hips and butt like I wanted my hands to. Compelled, I moved to touch her knees. I slid my hands upward along the silky skin of her legs and traced the curve to her inner thighs.

"No, no." She gave me a playful smirk. "I've told you already, Christopher. You can't have me until you've satisfied your rage."

"Please." I sucked air into my quivering mouth, hungry for the taste of her flesh. My body felt like it had only become the taste of juices that flowed into my throat and the throbbing sensation of my blood-filled member that threatened to split the fabric of my briefs.

She stared at me through the slits of her eyelids and hummed a sound. "You poor thing. You're killing me." She laughed. "You can kiss me." She tapped the mound between her legs. "Here. Over the fabric of my underwear. But that's it. A little tease before the real thing when you can show me that you're man enough to have me, of course." Her expression twisted into the beckoning smile of a sinister succubus.

I crawled onto the bed, trapping her legs beneath my body. I lowered my head until her taunting scent swirled in my nostrils. Electricity jolted downward through my thighs to weaken my knees. If I even brushed myself against her, I would probably come.

Then, a knock at my front door interrupted our important moment.

I cursed and slammed a fist into the mattress. I dragged my palm along the length of my face. The audacity of whomever came to my door at this hour chewed at my stomach with teeth of frustration beyond their understanding. Then my eyes widened with realization. I snapped my head upward. "The *necklace.*"

"Looks like I was wrong earlier," said Angelina's Maria.

I quickly, almost frantically, retrieved a bath robe from my closet and slipped it on. And my quick flight downstairs to peer through the peephole did not disappoint.

Mark stood on my porch with his hands plunged into the pockets of his hoodie that draped nearly to his sweatpants-hidden mid-thighs. Unsurprisingly slobbish.

I opened the door and greeted him cordially.

"Hey, man," he said. I wanted to roll my eyes. "I left that necklace on my dresser. My head's a little scattered, I guess. Just wanted to drop by and leave it with you, as promised." He gave me a half-smile.

I squirmed as he shuffled his hands inside his hoodie pocket to produce the jewelry. How disrespectful. This necklace was of utmost importance, and he couldn't even deliver it in a proper box.

"I wish I could stick around," he said, placing the necklace into my open and waiting palm. "But I'm headed to my sister's for a few nights. Hoping the family time will clear my head." He shrugged. "How are you doing?"

"Oh, I'm..." I shifted and felt my still half-erect penis against my thigh. And I then looked downward and away and sighed. "I'm doing okay, I suppose. Are you sure you don't want to come in for a quick glass of wine?"

"I really can't. I'm sorry."

"I'm sure you could use it." I gently caressed the chain and pendant, gazing at its shimmering beauty beneath the glow of the porch light. "It'd take the edge off. You've been through a lot."

He looked over my shoulder into my house, undoubtedly checking for Angelina.

"I sure could use the company," I continued. "It has been a rough night." I frowned and looked into his eyes.

"You know what?" He gave me a gentle smile. "I'll come in for one. Just one, and then I've gotta head out."

I returned his expression and stepped aside. With a sweeping gesture, I welcomed him to come inside. He stepped past me.

I poured him a glass of wine and left him to wait patiently for me at the kitchen table while I went to retrieve Angelina. And when I returned arm-in-arm with her, his eyes widened, and he seemed to choke on his wine.

"I hope you don't mind her presence, Mark," I said. "She likes to spend time with the company."

He gave her an awkward smile and waved lazily. A disrespectful salutation riddled with discomfort, as I would expect from him. "She looks...uh, she looks great, man. Those clothes really suit her." His eyes scanned her body up and down. I wondered if he saw the Maria in her that I did. I hoped it ignited an inferno of guilt in his gut.

I smiled. "She appreciates your kind words." I poured a glass of wine for myself and set it on the table. Then I walked to return the bottle back to the counter behind Mark.

"You're not going to do anything this time," Angelina whispered. "Are you?"

I gave her a glance, but I didn't answer. I walked to the table to grab the necklace.

"You're going to let him go again," she continued.

When I leaned to clasp the chain behind her neck, I whispered into her ear, "Just watch," and kissed her cheek.

I reached my trembling hand to grip the neck of the wine bottle. Fear kissed the mouth of exhilaration. I salivated. My heart pounded in my ears. My knuckles turned white as I gripped tighter against the threat of dropping the weapon from my sweating palms.

I took a deep, shaken breath.

"Hurry up." Angelina sounded giddy. "He's going to see you if you take any longer."

In one swift motion, I raised the bottle and swung. And it made contact with the back of Mark's head.

Glass rocketed across the kitchen like shrapnel. Mark grunted. His forehead thudded against the table as he slumped. Red wine mixed with the blood from his fresh head wound and rolled downward along his neck and shoulders.

"Wow." Angelina's tone carried the obvious weight of disbelief. "I didn't think you actually had the balls."

I didn't look at her. I just kept staring at Mark with a grin on my face and a tremble that wouldn't stop harassing my body.

"The job isn't finished yet, though."

I waited a moment, taking in the quiet and observing the object of my hatred. His back rose and fell with shallow breathing, but he didn't make a sound. I'd knocked him unconscious.

I grinned, and then panic began its assault. What would I do with him now? My eyes fell on the knife set on the counter.

"You'd better figure something out." A giggle followed her words. "Or he's going to wake up."

I glared. "He's out cold," I growled. "He likely has a concussion."

"Just dig the jagged edge of that bottle into his neck."

I looked at the toothy glass, wine still dripping from its edges. "No," I said. "I want to draw it out. That's too quick. And it'd leave too much of a mess in my kitchen."

She scoffed. "Are you making excuses?"

"No. I'm saying that if I want to marvel at my work, I don't want to have to clean it all up immediately."

"Fair enough." She shrugged.

The corners of my mouth tugged into another smile while I watched my unconscious victim lie still. And I knew what I would do with him.

I FOUGHT TO CATCH my breath. I didn't realize how heavy a person was. And I'd likely done unintended damage as Mark's head bounced off each step on my way into the basement with him. I hoped that he would still wake up.

Angelina watched as I put the finishing touches on the restraints that bound Mark to the weight bench. A steak knife waited for me on the floor. I grabbed it and began carefully cutting off his clothes. I didn't want to cut him on accident—I wanted to savor each conscious and intended tear into his flesh.

He squirmed as I finished. I stood.

"What the fuck?" he mumbled. His eyes rolled with delirium, and he lifted his head for a moment before it fell again.

"Well," I said. An uncontrollable smile cut into my cheeks. I almost giggled. "I am glad you're here with us now." I walked over to him and gently dragged the tip of the knife against the skin of his back.

He arched his back, attempting to lurch away from the blade, and made a moaning sound.

"Now, now." I dragged the blade against his scalp. "You can squirm all you want, but the inevitability of your pain is inescapable." Excitement forced giddy laughter from my mouth. "And the inevitability of your death is going to come a lot sooner than you thought."

He struggled again, pulling against his restraints with new vigor. His face twisted with the beginnings of a sob. "Why are you doing this to me, Chris?" His voice cracked. "I brought you what you wanted. I just want to see my sister."

I stepped back from him and slowly removed my bathrobe to reduce limb restriction. "There are things that we've all wanted and couldn't have. Right now, you want safety. Maria wanted to have a family with you."

"Is that what this is ab—"

I slammed an open hand against the center of his back as hard as I could. He gasped and coughed. "I wasn't finished." I swung one leg over him to straddle his body. I could feel the warmth of his ass through the thin layer of fabric of my briefs.

"Please," he begged. "Please, just stop this." I could see him straining to turn his head and shift his eyes to look at me.

"Chris," said Angelina in Maria's voice. "Keep going, baby. Please kill him for me."

I turned my head to look at her. My Maria. My lip quivered beneath her gaze. "Maria," I whispered. I clenched my jaw and gritted my teeth, and I turned back to Mark. I gripped the sides of his head and shoved his face against the weight bench. "I wanted to be with Maria. *I* would have given her the family she wanted." I grated my words through my teeth.

He squirmed against my grip, but the restraints took too much away from the strength he could have applied against me. I laughed in my dominance.

"Yes," moaned Maria. I looked over to see that she had tucked her hand between her legs. She slid her fingers over her cloth-covered slit. "You're so close to having this. So close. Keep going." I felt my cock hardening as I watched her.

I turned back to my struggling victim. I dug the tip of the knife into the flesh of his back and basked in the glory of his scream. "I *didn't* want Maria to die." I began carving the 'M' to begin her name. "But she killed herself because of *you*."

The rapid rise and fall of his chest made my carving difficult. He wound up to speak, and I dug the knife again to begin an 'A'. He shrieked again.

"*You took her from me*," I screamed. My eyes filled with tears.

"Chris," Mark said between breaths. "She didn't kill herself." He sucked in air against the pain.

"Don't you fucking lie to me, you piece of shit." Spit flew from my mouth onto his bleeding wounds. I carved an 'R'.

"Chris, please. She had an aneurysm."

I leaned over him, pressing my body against his. I put my mouth against his ear. "If she did, then it was because of the stress you put her through." I sat back up and began carving an 'I', and then an 'A'.

I stood and stepped back to admire my canvas. The man's back was a mess of bloody handprints and trails and smears. I laughed at his agony. I reveled in it. I wished I'd nicked an artery, because I craved to dance in its spurting.

I smiled when I realized that the time was coming.

I slipped my briefs down the length of my legs and stepped out of them. I approached my Maria and pressed my hardness against her. "Soon," I shakingly whispered. I ran a bloody hand over her lips. "You will have what you wanted, and I will have what I *need*. What I've been craving for so long." I wiped a tear from my cheek before I returned to my burning anger. "But first." I walked back over to Mark and straddled myself over his body again.

"Chris, listen to me." He sucked air through his teeth. I know his back seared in pain as his skin stretched with his breathing and talking. "I need you to listen to me."

"As if you deserve my audience." I tossed my knife onto the floor and then gripped his ass cheeks to spread them. The scent of unwashed orifice and sweat filled the room.

"*Please,*" he shrieked, trying to escape my assault.

I slid my body upward along the backs of his legs.

He clenched in protest.

"I'm going to give you what you refused her." I pressed against him to enter. "And then I'm going to slice open your throat like a gutted fish."

He slithered forward and away.

"Chris, this isn't what Maria would want." He rolled his body back and forth to prevent my invasion. "Think about it for a second."

"As if you'd know anything about what she'd want."

"Chris, I do. I *lived* with her. For years." He grunted and slid as far forward as he could. "*That's* not Maria." He nodded toward the Maria that stood and watched, who'd now slowed in her masturbation and glared at me.

"Don't you fucking stop, Christopher," growled Angelina in her own voice now.

"Maria *loved* me. *Think.*"

I backed myself away from him.

"*Kill him*," screamed Angelina. "*Now.*"

I remembered the tears in Maria's eyes when she spoke about Mark's mistreatment. The pain that wafted from her like a vulgar scent twisted my stomach to hatred. A pain of wanting to be loved by someone that couldn't seem to. Or never would. At least, not in the way you wanted them to.

I knew that pain.

That's not Maria.

I stood up.

"What are you doing, baby?" Angelina mimicked Maria again. "Don't you want me anymore?" She put on a fake display of crying.

I looked at the pile of weights stacked next to my weight bench. I bent forward and lifted one in each hand. Then I looked down over Mark. "I'll let you go." My tone was devoid of emotion.

Everything was over. Maria was dead. There'd be no having her. Whether she killed herself or not. And Angelina was no worthy substitute. None of this mattered. And she certainly would not have encouraged me to kill the man she loved. And I'd never have been that man, no matter how much I wanted myself to be.

"Think about what you're doing, Chris. They'll never let you see the light of day again. Don't you want me, even just for one night?"

I approached Angelina. "You are nothing but a wish." I clapped my weight laden hands together with her head between them. Plastic crunched and collapsed. I grabbed the mannequin and slammed it against the cold concrete floor. I stomped on Angelina's remains again and again until she was nothing but a mangled mess of shining white.

Then, someone pounded on my front door to interrupt me.

"Stay here," I said to Mark. "And be quiet. And I'll let you go."

He didn't say a word to me as I trudged up the stairs. I moved through the living room and opened the front door. "What can I do for you?" I said to the two uniformed police officers that greeted me.

Their expressions turned to concern. Their eyes scanned my body, and they looked at my hands. "We got a call from a concerned sister about the well-being of her brother." The officer that spoke dramatically chewed his gum and raised an eyebrow. "Says he never showed up tonight and might be in some emotional distress. She said he was coming here. You wouldn't know anything about that, would you?" Sarcasm painted his tone.

"No, I—"

Muffled screams for help seeped through my living room carpet.

"Okay," said the other officer as he stepped across my threshold.

I didn't fight the handcuffs that strangled my wrists.

The other police officer headed toward my basement door.

About Ronald J. Murray

Ronald J. Murray is a writer of speculative fiction and poetry living in Pittsburgh, Pennsylvania. His published work includes his two dark poetry collections, Cries to Kill the Corpse Flower, which appeared on the 2020 Bram Stoker Awards® preliminary ballot, the Wonderland Book Awards preliminary ballot, and was nominated for an Elgin Award, and Lost Letters to a Lover's Carcass, which appeared on the Wonderland Book Awards preliminary ballot. He curated and co-edited Verse Infernal: Poetry Inspired by the Satanic Religion from Aperient Press.

His short fiction and poetry has appeared in Space and Time Magazine, The Horror Writers Association's Poetry Showcase Volume VIII, on The Wicked Library Podcast, Ellen Datlow's Recommendations for Best Horror #14, in Bon Appetit: Stories and Recipes for Human Consumption, Lustcraftian Horrors: Erotic Stories Inspired by H.P. Lovecraft, and more. He is an Active Member of the Horror Writers Association.

ACKNOWLEDGEMENTS

The author would like to thank the following for their support throughout the production of this book:

My wife, Sarah, and our two boys. You inspire me to continue creating every single day, whether you realize it or not. For that, I couldn't be more thankful.

My parents and siblings, Gwenn, Ron, Ashley, Stephanie, and Nicholas, who buy, read, and rave about every piece I ever produce. I hope I make you all proud with the things that I create, even though some of it may be uncomfortable for you to read!

My mother-in-law, Barb, who puts up with my shit.

My Uncle Erik, who keeps asking me to put him in my acknowledgments (but he is very supportive of what I do).

All my colleagues in the field with me, who've had an amazing impact on me: Michael A. Arnzen, Sara Tantlinger, Candace Nola, Corey Niles, Gwendolyn Kiste, Jennifer Wilson, Douglas Gwilym, Nelson W. Pyles, Don Noble, Joshua Gage, Josh Malerman, Jeffrey Oliver, Rick Powell, Hydra Morningstar, Chelsea Warrington, Lisa Lebel, Jessica McHugh, Stephanie M. Wytovich, Nicholas Day, and many more.

Finally, my thanks go to the team at Uncomfortably Dark Horror, who made this book possible.

Episodes of Violence by David Bernstein. An extreme horror novel that contains graphic depictions of violence, sex, and gore.

Cremated Remains by M Ennenbach. A short story collection containing ten tales curated in the flames of madness, friendship, love, betrayal, and desire.

Order signed copies and limited-edition hardcovers from the shop:
https://www.uncomfortablydark.com/shop

Join our Patreon for free books, merch, and more!
https://www.patreon.com/user/membership?u=12231330&view
_as=patron